I0541039

The Rescuer and Other Science Fiction Stories

Other book collections by Arthur Porges:

Three Porges Parodies and a Pastiche (1988)
The Mirror and Other Strange Reflections (2002)
Eight Problems in Space: The Ensign De Ruyter Stories (2008)
The Adventures of Stately Homes and Sherman Horn (2008)
The Calabash of Coral Island and Other Early Stories (2008)
The Miracle of the Bread and Other Stories (2008)
Spring, 1836: Selected Poems (2008)
The Devil and Simon Flagg and Other Fantastic Tales (2009)
The Curious Cases of Cyriack Skinner Grey (2009)
The Ruum and Other Science Fiction Stories (2010)

Forthcoming titles by Arthur Porges:

Unusual Plants of the Galaxy
The Price of a Princess: Hardboiled Crime Fiction
Collected Essays: Volume One
Collected Essays: Volume Two

Books by F. W. Thomas (from the same publisher):

Tales From Stonecutter Street (2010)
Star Turns (2011)
The Rising Sap (2013)

The Rescuer and Other Science Fiction Stories

Arthur Porges

Edited by Richard Simms

Richard Simms Publications

This paperback first edition published in 2014

Richard Simms Publications, Surrey, England

ISBN: 978-0-9556942-9-5

Copyright © 2014 The Estate of Arthur Porges

Introduction Copyright © 2014 Richard Simms

All rights reserved

No part of this book may be reproduced in any form, or by any means, without prior permission in writing from the publisher.

With special thanks to Cele Porges and Joel Hoffman.

For more information please visit The Arthur Porges Fan Site:

http://arthurporges.atwebpages.com

Contents

Introduction

In my previous collection of Arthur Porges' science fiction, I assembled those stories that first appeared in magazines throughout the 1950s. Several of those were sold to his mentor Anthony Boucher at *The Magazine of Fantasy and Science Fiction*. It is my pleasure now to present to Porges fans everywhere this companion volume, which collects the bulk of his science fiction output from the following decade.

The 1960s proved to be a highly productive period in the author's writing career. Dozens of his short stories were published in a variety of (mostly monthly) American periodicals that specialized in the genres of science fiction, fantasy, mystery and detection—as well as the odd literary story sold to *Argosy* or the lucrative "men's" magazines that were so popular in this era.

By the start of the decade Porges had retired from his job as a college math teacher, teamed up with the Scott Meredith Literary Agency, and established himself as a full-time freelance writer of genre short fiction. Some of his best tales had indeed already been reprinted and preserved in book form. But many really good stories (not just from the 1950s, but throughout his career) never made it into anthologies; a lamentable fact that provides the main inspiration behind my ongoing series of Porges collections.

I hope readers of this present book will agree that the stories gathered here (including one that has never seen publication before) are worth another airing and showcase a writer at the height of his powers. As Arthur noted in one of his letters to me, the early 1960s in particular were a remarkably productive time for him: "I was a literary oyster back then!"

A short word about what is not included in this volume. In 2008 I edited *Eight Problems in Space*, which was published by The Battered Silicon Dispatch Box in Canada. That book collected all of Porges' Ensign De Ruyter stories; an exciting series of science fiction adventures that blended rollicking space opera with the kind of classic "scientific problem" yarn you might come across in an old issue of *Astounding Science Fiction* magazine. Although the Ensign De Ruyter stories appeared in *Amazing Stories* and *Fantastic* during the 1960s, I have elected not to reprint them again. At the time of writing, *Eight Problems in Space* is still available from the publisher and is recommended to anyone who enjoys this book.

Moreover, a small number of other tales that might have made it into this collection also proved to be ineligible for inclusion here—the issue this time being one of genre definitions. Considering that Porges penned a good deal of fantasy as well as science fiction, a number of his stories (dare I say even a few of those presented here!) could be seen as a mixture of both genres. It's an old fashioned phrase, but I have often thought the term "science fantasy" could be applied to many of Porges' crossover speculative/weird tales.

Can one be overly concerned about these labels? I must admit to being as guilty as anyone of worrying too much over defining which genre a particular story belongs to—some simply defy categorization. But for all that, a recent look at the stories Mike Ashley included in his collection of Arthur's supernatural fiction *The Mirror and Other Strange Reflections* (Ash-Tree Press, 2002) gave me pause for thought. I was amused to see there are several I would probably have classed as science fiction and included in this book: "The Radio," "The Fanatic," and "The Moths." This kind of hairsplitting is of course not that important. As with *Eight Problems in Space*, Mike Ashley's superb anthology is still in print—these days you can even download it in e-book format, although I prefer a "real" book over one of those every time!

Before I go on to discuss the individual stories collected here, I wish to share some thoughts about my introductory essay to the previous science fiction collection, *The Ruum and Other Science Fiction Stories* (2010). In that commentary I remarked that Porges wrote a good deal in the sub-genre of "hard" science fiction, a statement that at least one person has taken issue with. It is true that Arthur's quirky storytelling style and ideas are pretty far removed (and do not share the same scope and breadth of vision) from the expansive writings of the great "hard" science fiction exponents Hal Clement and Raymond F. Jones, both of whom were contemporaries of Porges. However, I do think there is enough meticulously researched science and attention to detail in a typical story by the latter in this genre for the term "hard" science fiction to apply to at least some of his output. Indeed, a quintessential Arthur Porges plot is solely built around a certain scientific fact—or more specifically a well thought out extrapolation of a particular item of established scientific knowledge that the author had at his disposal.

Furthermore, as my friend the literary researcher Morgan Wallace points out, we all have our own personal ideas of what defines "hard" science fiction. One could submit that Porges' work does not belong to this sub-genre because his tales are unlike those of Hal Clement. But is that not akin to stating a story cannot be considered a planetary romance if it is written in a different style to that of Leigh Brackett?

I may be dazzling the reader with penetrating analysis or tying myself up in knots here. I'm not sure which. It goes without saying that the genre as a whole is a broad spectrum. The purist's counter argument is illustrated by a quote from Basil Wells, who is incidentally one of my favorite authors: "Science fiction, in its purest sense, should mean entertaining and colorful fiction that either extrapolates what logically, or possibly, will take place in the future."

Now for the stories themselves. Porges continued to sell his work to *The Magazine of Fantasy and Science Fiction* in the 1960s, although by the start of the decade Anthony Boucher's editorship had come to an end. I have decided to open this collection with two absolute gems from that journal, the first of which is "A Specimen for the Queen" (1960). This little known and never reprinted tale is in fact the long lost sequel to "The Ruum" (1953), the author's most celebrated story. It is a bit of a mystery as to why this tongue-in-cheek follow up, which Arthur and myself agreed was pretty good, didn't take off.

So for those who wondered what ever happened to the ruum after its dealings with Jim Irwin (the prospector in the first story), here it is! Indeed, there is a lovely, fleeting reference to Irwin early on in the sequel, where the ruum's robotic brain recalls a "certain encounter with an elusive biped." The story is set some years after the events described in "The Ruum." The narrative opens with the specimen-collecting robot still in the Canadian Rockies, having dutifully gathered all the lifeforms available that fit the weight ratio setting given to it by the long dead aliens that accidentally left the robot behind million of years ago in Earth's history.

Enter into this setting another spaceship that lands in the vicinity, an exploratory vessel manned by a crew which are members of an extraterrestrial race of bee-people who are technologically advanced but morally bereft—sadistic, even. On discovering the ruum, they mistake it for a typical native species and set about trying to capture it as a specimen for the ruler of their home planet.

Suffice to say the aliens soon realize they have made a huge error of judgement in imprisoning the ruum and taking it with them into outer space. As the story progresses there is much comedy as well as a certain grim irony for the reader to enjoy as the crew's bewilderment at the robot's apparent indestructibility turns to panic. I love the story's ending and I am delighted to rescue "A Specimen for the Queen" from obscurity by reprinting it here.

Reprinted only the once and from the same publication is "Turning Point" (1965). We travel to a possible future Earth for this one, a very different world where after a devastating nuclear war, mankind is under the control of intelligent rats. When I first read this story years ago, I thought of it as an unacknowledged sequel to Porges' earlier classic science fiction yarn "The Rats" (1951). I put this to Arthur during our correspondence. He replied that he hadn't written "Turning Point" as a conscious follow up to "The Rats," going on to remark that it was one of those stories of his that championed the indomitable human spirit. Porges felt strongly that even if 99% of us were to be killed, a small number of us would survive and rise again, averring that "we are a hard species to wipe out!"

The following four stories in this book have been drawn from the pages of John W. Campbell's *Analog* magazine; formerly *Astounding Science Fiction*, before it changed title in 1960. It is mildly surprising that none of Porges' stories, which at least bordered on "hard" science fiction, appeared in *Astounding Science Fiction* in the 1950s. The first piece to make it into this prestigious, renamed journal was "The Rescuer" (1962), a startling story that has been anthologized several times since its original appearance—Brian Aldiss was an admirer who was instrumental in ensuring Arthur's tale gained a deservedly wider exposure. Porges may have been happily detached from the genre's mainstream, a recluse who avoided science fiction conventions and was content to follow a unique career path and his own particular niche. But "The Rescuer" certainly made readers and editors stand up and take notice.

It's a time travel yarn that meditates on the paradoxes that arise when one journeys back in history and attempts to alter the past—an idea already well explored in a variety of ways by other writers in the years before "The Rescuer" was written. What sets apart Porges' take on this theme (and surely explains the enduring appeal it has to this day) is the thought provoking, theological angle.

The story is told in the form of a courtroom hearing, with two scientists being called upon by the judge to explain why they took it upon themselves to destroy a top secret, newly invented time machine owned by the US government. As the justification for their sabotage becomes clear at the denouement, we are left with a very provocative story indeed. The defendants had discovered that a religious fanatic armed with a repeat action rifle had gained access to the machine and intended to travel back in time 2,000 years to the Golgotha Plains in order to prevent the Crucifixion. They argue that such an action would change history utterly, and not necessarily for the better, raising the question of what the alternative future world would be like if Christianity had never existed. In the end, circumstances dictated that their decision had to be taken quickly, rightly or wrongly. With sublime effect, the narrative is left cleverly open-ended. The fact that the author was a lifelong atheist also gives "The Rescuer" a certain paradoxical appeal and it is certainly one of Porges' most affecting stories.

The elegantly written "Problem Child" (1964) has a much quieter theme, that of a widowed professor who is unable to communicate with his retarded, three-year-old son. The idea Arthur explores here is that somehow, in the rarefied atmosphere of higher mathematics, the two can achieve a meeting of minds. It's a beautiful concept that is dealt with sensitively. One can see why this story has already been reprinted elsewhere. Porges was especially fond of this one.

In the field of mystery fiction, Arthur had a penchant for writing stories that featured sleuths known for their lateral thinking; Sherlock Holmes-inspired characters with the ability to solve "impossible" crimes that have baffled the detectives who solicit their help. In this tradition, except without the criminous element, the next three stories follow the cerebral exploits of one Dr. Corman, a Cal Tech man known for befuddling one of his colleagues by demonstrating scientific gimmicks straight out of left field. Engineers by trade, the two men jostle with each other (not always good-naturedly) in the area of amateur biology. The tone of these stories is light and the crisp dialogue between the two scientists as they pit their wits against each other makes for humorous reading. My favorite in this short series is "The Topper" (1963), in which Corman tricks his skeptical colleague into believing he has discovered a colony of intelligent cockroaches in his kitchen! Similarly ingenious hoaxes are on display in the other two Corman stories.

This trio of entertaining diversions first appeared during 1963, "The Topper" and "Controlled Experiment" in *Analog* magazine and "The Formula" in *Amazing Stories*. The latter is the first of several Porges stories I have presented here that are drawn from that Ziff-Davis owned monthly publication and its companion magazine, *Fantastic*.

In the early 1960s, Cele Goldsmith was in the midst of her celebrated editorial reign at the helm of these two periodicals. High praise has rightly been bestowed on her for publishing offbeat short fiction by a loose conglomeration of fresh young talents. Goldsmith was brave enough to buy the infamous Moderan stories by David R.

Bunch; a series widely acknowledged as a seminal masterpiece today but disliked at the time by a number of readers of the two magazines, rightly referred to since as "schmucks" by Harlan Ellison! Then there were Robert F. Young's poetic, visionary tales, and of course Porges himself offering up dozens of fantasy and science fiction stories, the former of which myself and Mike Ashley have collected in book form elsewhere.

With *Analog's* leanings towards "hard" science fiction, and *The Magazine of Fantasy and Science Fiction's* aspirations to being a more literary journal than its competitors in the digest-sized fiction magazine market, it was perhaps left to Goldsmith's titles to carry on with the old pulp traditions of florid prose and adventure. To go against this viewpoint, older writers like Edmond Hamilton, who found a new market for their work in *Amazing Stories* and *Fantastic*, were penning some of their most mature, accomplished stories. I am thinking of such wonderful pieces by Hamilton as "Requiem" and "Sunfire," both from 1962 and two true classics of the genre that surely transcended much of his earlier work for the pulps.

In addition, it should be admitted that Goldsmith published a good deal of avant-garde, experimental writing as well by the aforementioned Bunch and other cavalier authors; much of this material was in keeping with the "New Wave" revolution that dominated science fiction literature at the time.

Returning to the stories in this collection, I would never describe Porges' 1960s science fiction as "New Wave." He would probably have laughed at that! However, pieces like "Degree Candidate," printed under the pseudonym "Peter Arthur" in the January 1961 issue of *Fantastic*, are certainly different, to say the least.

The plot of this story is highly unusual and hard to summarize without giving too much away. A gifted student faces a board of examiners in a meeting to determine the questionable morality of his recent experiments. To attend the conference in person, young Jav must permit "energy to flow in vibrant quanta through certain networks of his complex, multidimensional structure." In this manner Porges deftly informs the reader that the characters in his tale are not of this Earth but non-organic beings able to communicate by thought alone and comprised solely of electrical energy.

"Degree Candidate" is one of his most imaginative works, a story about higher intelligences that are able to create, manipulate and destroy entire planets and their inhabitants. The idea at its core develops into a typically idiosyncratic exploration of Arthur's own belief that were there an omnipotent, godlike entity watching over us all it would hardly be benevolent. A subsequent issue of *Fantastic* carried a disapproving letter by a reader who felt that with such an unorthodox take on Creation, whoever wrote under the byline of "Peter Arthur" was guilty of blasphemy. The editor did not agree with the reader's sentiments and the author himself was merely amused!

As I have noted in previous introductions, Porges' main strength as a writer was his gift for utilizing an obscure fact, usually from the realm of science, and using this as the basis for a story. In essence he was, as Mike Ashley so neatly put it, an ideas man.

The ingenious idea behind "The Auto Hawks" (1960), partly inspired by his love of ornithology, is pure Porges. The setting is the area around the Santa Ana Hills in Southern California which, incidentally was where Arthur was living at the time this story was written. Oversized hawks have taken to preying on automobiles in the region; their swooping attacks over the freeways making it apparent the birds see cars as a source of food. The depictions of the local population's reaction to this phenomenon and the efforts of the authorities to combat the threat of the mutated falcons are written with both realism and wit. Who else could have thought up a story with such a bizarre premise, then in a step-by-step manner logically rationalized the whole idea? The persuasive explanation at the conclusion lends "The Auto Hawks" a certain this-could-actually-happen frisson.

Staying with the Ziff-Davis magazines, "Revenge" (1961) and "Off His Rocker" (1960), are from *Amazing Stories* and *Fantastic* respectively. Both stories are narrated by talented but dangerously unhinged research scientists. "Revenge" is a clever, dark story told by an angry biochemist who has found an ingenious method of solving the problem of the illicit trade in narcotics. His groundbreaking, practical solution to the war on drugs and the toppling of the organized crime syndicates is, as Porges' thoughtful tale progresses, lost in a welter of government bureaucracy, disbelief and the unwillingness of authority to act. Politicians and officialdom are evidently too intertwined with the drug trafficking cartels to make use of his idea or go down the road of decriminalization.

This absorbing story has echoes of Arthur Selling's marvelous novel "The Quy Effect" (1967), which likewise is a tale of a scientist ahead of his time who nobody believes. As with Sellings, Porges takes wry potshots at society in general, not just the powers-that-be, but the general public whom he argues is as much to blame for the epidemic of substance abuse as any statesman or bureaucrat.

Another scientific genius vents his frustrations in "Off His Rocker," which is lighter in tone but equally innovative. Having his inventions in the realms of gravitation and electromagnetism ridiculed in the pages of a local newspaper, an amateur scientist devises a unique method of retribution against the proprietors of that publication. After putting together a vibrating contraption that works on the principle of resonance, the embittered narrator installs his device in the newspaper's headquarters building, setting off an earthquake which to his horror he realizes he is unable to stop—the intention had been to bring down only the one structure. I have always been fond of this story, although when I complimented Arthur on it he disagreed. I believe he felt it was just a potboiler and not very realistic. But I like it, anyway!

A fair amount of older science fiction is of course anachronistic; the science in much of the genre can become dated with time. At first glance this is the case with the otherwise well written "Mulberry Moon" (1961). As with the previous two stories, it involves the exploits of gifted scientists. Walt Tremayne and Marshall Elder have devised a new super-fluorescent substance that the US government wishes to use in a rocket they intend to send crashing into the moon's crust. The idea is that the chemical agent in the cone of the spacecraft will make the collision with the lunar surface visible to observers on Earth.

The effect this event has on our planet's satellite is unexpected and one of Porges' most original ideas, through which he makes a startling guess at the nature of the moon's origin. Unfortunately, when one considers that eight years after "Mulberry Moon" was published Neil Armstrong uttered those immortal words, the tale does seem rather quaint. Nevertheless, on rereading Arthur's yarn for the purposes of this collection, I was struck by how good it still is: snappy dialogue, fascinating science, and a wonderful idea that fuels the plot and could even have relevance today.

Consider the late Sir Patrick Moore's assertion (so sad he is no longer with us) that there is still much we do not know about the moon. And consider also our new awareness about organisms being able to exist and thrive in extreme environments hitherto thought to be unable to sustain life. Moreover, Porges' speculation about the moon doesn't seem quite so wacky when one bears in mind that it is now seriously theorized in scientific circles that life on Earth may have originated from bacteria carried across space to our planet by meteorites, possibly from Mars. Fifty years ago, when "Mulberry Moon" was amusing the readership of *Fantastic* magazine, *that* idea would have been the subject of general ridicule.

There is a lyricism about "The Melanas" (1960). It's one of the most beautifully written and poignant stories in the Porges science fiction canon and one of the very few that is set on a planet in another solar system. For several centuries a group of human settlers have led a pastoral existence on an enchanting, idyllic world. The melanas are the only native lifeform that could conceivably do the community any harm. Despite the fact that this peace-loving population has coexisted with these indigenous creatures for so many years, the latter appear to serve no purpose in the ecology of the planet and are ravaging the farmers' crops. A sudden blood lust enters the soul of the people, who become intent on wiping out them out entirely. In this, perhaps Arthur was reflecting on mankind's latent, natural killer instinct. To be frank, if "The Melanas" carries a message at all it is surely somewhat misanthropic.

The lone voice of reason in this madness is the poet Caslor, who senses intuitively that to exterminate an entire species to the point of extinction would have dire consequences for the human colony. His Cassandra-like warnings, perhaps inevitably, go unheeded. When it was published, "The Melanas" mirrored what had entered the public consciousness at the time: an increasing disquiet over mankind's destruction of his environment. In that sense this tale is very much of its day. Then again, the story's sentiment is still relevant, with concerns about conservation and global warming now at the forefront of the political agenda.

For the next story we leave behind the wealth of material Arthur sold to the Cele Goldsmith titles. Porges placed a number of his works in *Bizarre! Mystery Magazine*, an excellent publication that printed a mixed bag of short fiction across several genres. I have reprinted his only science fiction story for that magazine here. "A Civilized Community" (1965) is out of the top drawer, a masterful piece that could reasonably be described as a "lost" classic. Never anthologized, it was in all likelihood missed at the time by connoisseurs of Arthur's science fiction.

A spaceship from another galaxy crash lands on Earth with only one survivor, a vulnerable, gentle natured insectoid being that possesses a keen intelligence. Finding itself in a hostile, dangerous environment, the odyssey our hapless visitor from another world undergoes is chronicled in this compelling tale as he falls prey to various species of predatory, native fauna. Unable to achieve telepathic communication with another lifeform on the same intellectual level, and with the odds of survival stacked against it, the shipwrecked alien physicist's doomed struggle to live makes for an exciting read.

"A Civilized Community" reminds me a little of "By A Fluke" (1955), one of the stories I included in the previous science fiction volume. Both tales paint a detailed picture of a creature gifted with intelligence but cursed with a vulnerable body—in the earlier piece the life span of the species is all too short. This last idea, clearly a pet theme of the author, is explored further in the following story, "Alien" (1964), a startling vignette even more similar to "By A Fluke" in that it also features a parasitic, sentient organism lacking motility. It appeared in the September, 1964 edition (complete with a photograph of Ursula Andress on the front cover!) of the somewhat racy "men's" periodical *Rascal*. Porges' contribution was singled out for high praise in the issue's editorial, with editor Frank Sorren remarking that it was one of the finest stories they had ever published.

Considering its provenance in a non-genre magazine and the fact that it was never reprinted, "Alien" is another rare science fiction gem I am pleased to present to a modern audience. Just what the alien entity, with its consciousness trapped inside a helpless body, actually *is* remains a mystery until the final paragraph. With the author inserting the odd tantalizing clue as to the being's true nature, astute readers may well make an accurate guess before the revelation at the end.

From the same magazine and year is "Irresistible Attraction" (1964). It's a haunting story that Arthur deemed to be one of his very best. As with "Alien," the importance of this tale has unfortunately been veiled by its appearance in a relatively ephemeral publication. The tone is dark in this classic science fiction drama set in the far future. Earth has been invaded and colonized by a superior race of aliens. Only a handful of the erstwhile dominant species is left; the few surviving, subjugated humans having degenerated into a semi-barbaric state. Raiding for food in one of the conquerors' agricultural plots, an unusually cunning scavenger (the aliens refer to humans as "grifs" in this story) evades capture and causes much consternation for two servants of the alien masters. The tale follows their discussion of the problem and the tactics they employ in endeavoring to ensnare the troublesome native. The solution, which I can hardly discuss here without spoiling the ending, is ingenious and concludes the story on a tragic note. I am thrilled to honor Arthur's memory by including "Irresistible Attraction" in this volume.

Previously unpublished, the uncompromisingly grim "Doomsday Incident" is a near-future tale about a dysfunctional family taking shelter in a bunker with the threat of atomic war imminent. The manuscript for this story dates from 1962; at the time Porges was savoring the writer's life, beachcombing and birdwatching in Laguna Beach. Where the inspiration for this somber piece came from I do not know, other than the obvious widespread fear of nuclear annihilation there was at the height of the Cold War. As to why "Doomsday Incident" never sold, one can surmise that editors might have found it a little too unsettling for their readers. It may not be one of the author's best, but I felt it an interesting enough footnote to his science fiction output to warrant inclusion here.

Rounding of this collection is the outstanding "Priceless Possession" (1966). Culled from an issue of *Galaxy* magazine, it is a little curious to note that this was his only sale to that publication. One would have thought Arthur's quirky and often humorous style made him well placed to become a regular contributor to *Galaxy*. Not that there is anything remotely light hearted about "Priceless Possession." It features one of his most imaginative creations, the Solar Sailor, which eagle-eyed fans will recall is mentioned in the Ensign De Ruyter story "Brain Slug." The S-2, as it is otherwise known, is an intelligent alien lifeform similar in body and shape to the Portuguese Man of War of Earth's oceans and able to live in the vacuum of interstellar space.

A three-man crew of an exploratory spacecraft, on a mission between the stars, encounters one of these extremely scarce and highly prized organisms. The Solar Sailor has long been assumed by mankind to be a "lower animal of inconsiderable consciousness" and therefore fair game to hunters who stand to make a fortune from the incredible properties of the creature's prized "sails." This is the part of the S-2 that enables it to drift for eons across the voids that separate galaxies by reacting to light, while finding sustenance by devouring cosmic dust in the manner of a whale ingesting plankton. As an aside, while acknowledging that the S-2 was a good idea, in a letter to me Porges admitted that such a creature could almost certainly not exist. He felt the idea behind its motion was still sound today, but the description of its physical make up was unfeasible and in all honesty the stuff of pure fantasy—attributing all those qualities to one organism was a tad far fetched!

The plot of "Priceless Possession" centers on the crew's reaction to their encounter with such a valuable animal. Although normally unable to communicate its thoughts to humans (hence the Solar Sailor's classification as a non-sentient being), the captain of the ship, under the influence of a strong drug, is rendered abnormally receptive and able pick up the S-2's mental emissions. Realizing the truth, he orders his disbelieving crewmates to allow the organism to give a clear, physical sign to prove beyond doubt it really is communicating telepathically with the captain and the latter is not just hallucinating. A moral quandary follows as the story works towards a horrifying conclusion.

David Drake reprinted this polished, melancholy tale in his anthology *Men Hunting Things* (1988). I found myself concurring with Drake's insightful comment on the story in his essay about Porges for the book *Twentieth Century Science Fiction Writers* (1986), wherein he reflected that the author was essentially stating that mankind's greatest enemy may not be external to our own hearts. I can put it no more eloquently than that.

"Priceless Possession" turned out to be one of the last stories Porges wrote in this genre for some years. In the 1970s he penned "Night of the Puppet," a strange fusion of science fiction and a police procedural detective story. It went unsold in an era when the market for short fiction was much reduced with so many of the genre magazines having been discontinued. "Night of the Puppet" remained unpublished until I was able to save it from oblivion by including it in the collection *The Miracle of the Bread and Other Stories* (2008).

In his later years Arthur focused more on writing mystery fiction, while redirecting much of his creative energy to the realm of poetry. He also contributed over forty feature articles to his local newspaper in the 1980s. Porges returned to the science fiction field the following decade, placing his "Unusual Plants of the Galaxy" series of vignettes (the reader may be interested to know that I plan to republish these in book form soon) in a fantastically obscure periodical called *Memo*. In the early 2000s he enjoyed something of a renaissance by selling a few science fiction and fantasy yarns to his old stomping ground *The Magazine of Fantasy and Science Fiction*, which had bought his first science fiction story back in 1951. This unexpected flourish was a burst of creativity that proved to be a swan song to a published writing career spanning half a century.

But I don't think Arthur would have minded my saying his most distinguished body of work in the science fiction medium appeared in the golden age of the 1950s and '60s. This is when it all happened: an explosion of originality and great storytelling resulting in the fascinating parade of entertaining tales assembled across these two volumes.

I love these stories and I hope you do too.

Richard Simms
Surrey, England
July, 2014

A Specimen for the Queen

PROLOGUE

The cruiser *Ilkor* had just gone into her interstellar overdrive beyond the orbit of Pluto when a worried officer reported to the Commander.

"Excellency," he said uneasily, "I regret to inform you that because of a technician's carelessness, a Type H-9 Ruum has been left behind on the third planet, together with anything it may have collected."

The Commander's triangular eyes hooded momentarily, but when he spoke his voice was level.

"How was the ruum set?"

"For a maximum radius of thirty miles, and 150 pounds plus or minus fifteen."

There was silence for several seconds, then the Commander said: "We cannot reverse course now. In a few weeks we'll be returning, and can pick up the ruum then. I do not care to have one of those costly self-energizing models charged against my ship. You will see," he ordered coldly, "that the individual responsible is severely punished."

But at the end of its run, in the neighborhood of Rigel, the cruiser met a flat, ring-shaped raider; and when the inevitable firefight was over, both ships, semi-molten, radioactive, and laden with dead, were starting a billion-year orbit around the star.

And on the Earth, it was the Age of Reptiles.

Ruum: The ultimate in a specimen-collecting robot. Self-energizing, it utilizes every known band of radiation to accumulate power. It is practically indestructible, the only regions barred to it being the interiors of stars. At present, some twenty types are officially authorized. Among these are ruums designed to collect specimens weighing from 0.001 pound to over fifty tons, at velocities beginning with inches per minute to miles per second*.

The spaceship landed on the daylight side of the Earth in a region of inhospitable, snowy peaks, deliberately bypassing the many big cities which showed up clearly on the screen, even at a thousand miles above the troposphere. This was standard procedure for a scout. The invariable policy of the bee-people was to snatch an isolated individual and retreat. The examination of their captive, carried out well away from its kind, could always be depended upon to type the opposition.

Naturally, with generations of colonizing behind them, the raiders knew enough to ignore the relatively unintelligent flora and fauna, which usually shared civilized worlds with their dominant forms. They looked for a lone specimen using power, or at least sophisticated tools, confident that it would be reasonably typical of the city building race. No attempt was ever made on this first snatch-and-run operation to approach any large community. Not through fear, of course, but merely to avoid alarming, and possibly alerting, their victims too soon—although this was routine caution, since a fleet of these scouts had ravaged the planets of a whole galaxy without a serious challenge to their superiority as fighting machines. The few races that had spaceships still floundered from one world to the next, and were no match for these heavily armed, interstellar raiders, assassins backed by hundreds of years of superb technology.

Although this was one of the bee-people's smallest scouts, it was set down boldly, with almost nonchalant arrogance. For one thing, while hovering far above a large city, they had detected only minor applications of atomic energy. The inference was obvious; this race was in its technological infancy compared with theirs. Consequently there was nothing whatever to fear.

"I wish," Captain Zril buzzed, "that we might find just one planet, *not* of the same old carbon cycle, that supports a new kind of life. Who could have guessed originally that all living things are oxygen breathers and confined to environments very nearly identical

---

* PRIMER OF ROBOTICS, Eighth Edition.

throughout the universe? A tiny variation in the upper ozone layer, a break in the nitrogen-bacterial cycle, and—*zzst!*—life ends. Oh, for something new."

He raised his 162 pounds of jointed body erect upon the last pair of legs, and with his four filmy wings dropping, sighed: "I suppose we may as well grab the usual so called intelligent being, if any, and leave. 'A Specimen for the Queen,' " he added, using the official phrase without irony, for the giant, immobile, egg-laying female was sacred to every bee. "We're about ready to go home, anyhow. Soon the colonizing armada will set out to subjugate all the suitable planets we found. I almost feel," he concluded wearily, "that it would be a relief to meet some lifeform high enough to give us just a little real opposition. How many generations has it been since our people fought a war?"

"We won't find one here," Lieutenant Briz said. "All I've seen in this area so far are subordinate species, ignorant of tools and power. Many of them are tiny, with wings. They couldn't possibly be responsible for those cities. Maybe the intelligent forms shun this part of the planet. If so, we might have to search elsewhere."

"Going home," Sergeant Srt shrilled, his thoughts still on the captain's remarks. "Am I glad this boring tour is about over. Tell you what, Lieutenant, I'll bet you my ration of honey that our last specimen screams more under the dissecting knife than that feathery quadruped from the second planet."

"Agreed," the lieutenant retorted instantly, his compound eyes alight with gluttony and malice. "You forgot, Sergeant, that it's my turn to use the knife. I'll see that he outdoes the quadruped. I have a flair, you know, and a profound knowledge of all types of nervous systems." At the sight of the sergeant's drooping palps, he buzzed with delight.

"That'll take some doing," the captain remarked. "How the feathery thing squalled ... You're not the only one who understands nerves," he rebuked Briz. "I—" He broke off as a sibilant call came from the fourth bee, on watch.

"Something interesting, sir," Technician Wrzs announced, gesturing towards the visiport. "Intelligent life, beyond a doubt. We won't have to look any further." He stepped aside respectfully as the captain approached. Peering through the glowing viewer, the commander saw a greyish object, quasi-spherical in shape, rolling along in a leisurely, almost contemplative manner. At the other visiport, his three subordinates watched with approval.

"Undoubtedly a vehicle of transport," the lieutenant assured his crew. "What do you read, Wrzs?"

"Not atomic, sir," the technician replied, studying the bank of dials.

"Could it be shielded?"

"Nothing that small could keep hard radiation in," Sergeant Srt volunteered. "A more primitive power source is indicated."

"In any case," the commander said with satisfaction, "there's a fairly advanced lifeform inside, and we'll soon have completed our mission. Then for home!"

"Seems a bit bored," the sergeant hummed. His palps quivered eagerly. "We'll cure that fast enough. When he's shucked out of his ingenious little vehicle, and our wager is being settled, life will become distinctly more interesting for him, although he'll be anxious enough to part with it! Shall I snatch the machine up with a force beam, sir?" he asked the captain.

"No. It may not even be necessary. See, he's studying us. Another of these naive races who expect to be treated as friends and equals. Don't grab him unless he runs."

The globular, leathery object was indeed examining the spaceship by means of lens-tipped rods and other more complex detectors, vaguely electronic in appearance. Finally, with an air of calm resolution, the ruum retracted all its instruments, and at a speed of five miles an hour, rolled towards the raider, assured that it held four creatures new to its collection, and of ideal mass. Although a ruum is obviously incapable of boredom, it is true that for many centuries there had been little left to do. Except for a certain encounter with an elusive biped twenty years earlier, life had been altogether routine. Prowling within its thirty-mile radius, the ruum was unable to find any new specimens in the 135-165 pound class to which its setting restricted the robot. When it had rounded out its gallery of preserved animals with a hairy chested, bearded, big-game hunter and writer, the ruum was reduced to aimless patrols and a vague electronic hoping. Its strange collection, like some fantastic butcher shop, included everything from small stegosaurs to man—every lifeform to be found in the Canadian Rockies since the age of reptiles. The region had been closed to humans for many years now, the government having wisely given up its attempts to destroy or even immobilize the incredible spheroid.

"Well," the lieutenant exclaimed cheerfully, "it's rolling right to the slaughter. It's going to be a pleasure to colonize this planet; I can see that. Shall I open the ramp to the specimen prison, sir? I wouldn't be surprised if the stupid thing came right in. I wonder," he mused happily, "if it will scream, bellow, whistle, growl, or buzz."

"Certainly not buzz," the captain reproved him. "Only the highest of the intelligent lifeforms buzz. They and the tiny insects we've found in a few places. And even the insects are advanced at least to the point of serving their race above all else. But yes, lower the ramp; this is specimen collecting in luxury."

The metal gangway swung smoothly into position, and without a moment's pause the ruum rolled up into the thick walled, well equipped laboratory. Soundlessly the massive door clicked shut behind it, and in the control room a hum of derisive laughter arose.

Now there is nothing devious about a ruum: it is a simple minded robot with a unique, though routine, job to be done. It is more subtle, in its operations, than a battering ram, since it takes the most direct measures called for, even though they may be relatively complex.

As a battery of bright lights—sodium, ultra-violet, infra-red, x-ray, and others unknown on Earth—illuminated the dissecting room in a preliminary survey of the raider's catch, the sphere extruded a few instruments of its own. It took only seconds for the robot to conclude that the specimens it needed were still out of reach. The ruum paused, took some bearings, and rolled to the North Bulkhead. That way—there—said its meters. Four 160-pound specimens you've never found before. You know what to do.

Meanwhile, Lieutenant Briz, filled with mild anticipation, was saying to the sergeant: "First I'll pry him out of the vehicle. What's the odds he's an air breather?"

"Not a fair bet, sir," the other protested. "A gilled animal wouldn't be running around on dry land so far from water. And what makes you think it's a 'he'? It might be a 'she' or an 'it.' "

"It's just a specimen to me. Who cares about the sex, if any, of vermin?"

"Makes a lot of difference to the other vermin," Srt said, unable to resist the chestnut.

Briz fluttered his palps in disgust.

"Remember those gill breathers on Lugar? Their craft were filled with water. Besides, there is a lake not far from here; we saw it before landing. However, enough gabble. Let's nip the thing with force beams and cut it open. If it needs water, or ice, or anything else, we can supply them fast enough to keep the specimen alive."

The ruum had halted by the North Wall, and as it stood there, the lieutenant pressed a stud. Five pale wands of pulsating energy converged on the musing globe. They saw dust puff from the warty surface. Another deft gesture by the officer, and a glittering circular saw glided out on a thick rocker arm to a point only inches from the ruum.

Seeming mildly surprised by all these maneuvers, the robot began extending an assortment of detectors. The captain gave a little buzz of astonishment.

"I could swear," he said wonderingly, "that it pushed one of those rods right through the second beam."

"Hardly likely, sir," Lieutenant Briz assured him calmly. "The torque on these rays is of the order—"

"I know all that, Briz," was the testy reply. "Are you trying to teach me engineering fundamentals? You're hardly out of the egg yet!"

The junior officer subsided into a limp, apologetic silence, his palps dangling.

"Well, well—" the captain ordered irritably. "Start the saw, Lieutenant, and let's get this over with."

There was a shrill, grating hum as the metal teeth came down hard against the ruum's armor. An incredulous silence followed. It had at least two good causes. One, the saw was obviously not cutting, in spite of the fact that it could slice the hardest alloys known to the bee-people at a rate of many inches per minute; and, two, the ruum had casually, almost insolently, rolled free of the five force beams, which had often pinned motionless great scaled beasts from many a planet. There were four simultaneous buzzes of amazement, ranging from thin, blowfly pitch to deep, menacing wasp notes.

"It—it—" Technician Wrzs babbled. "B—but those rays—they're—" He stopped, mandibles clashing with indignation, for the ruum had produced a whirling saw of its own, a glowing disc that flickered like a flame. Thrusting this tool forward on a flimsy looking rod, the ruum made a single lightning stroke, as if scribing a circle. There was a dull clang as a four-foot, mathematically perfect section of the thick metal wall fell out, leaving a neat, round orifice.

"Quick—it's going to get away!" the captain cried. "Stop it, you fools!" Then he snapped: "Sergeant, take the ship up to cruising height. The thing probably can't fly. We'll recapture it out in space where it can't leave." Even as he spoke, a second circular portion fell out, this time almost at their feet, and through the gap came the ruum, heading directly for the captain. In a matter of moments it had penetrated five thick bulkheads to reach them, and the viewer was no longer needed. The robot was now in the control room with the crew. Horrified, the four bees saw a gleaming, syringe-like probe, dripping greenish liquid, rise to working position on the sphere.

"Ray it, quick!" the captain ordered. "Forget about capturing it!"

Sergeant Srt, fastest of the group, had his handgun out in eight hundredths of a second. The potent bluish beam played squarely on the robot, and instantly the dust and debris on the surface was fiery slag. But the ruum kept coming. Only the milling about of the four bees had delayed its approach to the captain. A heavy explosive bullet from the lieutenant's animal gun jarred the control room with its vicious detonation without slowing the implacable sphere; and when Technician Wrzs, foolishly brave, swung at it with a heavy bar, the ruum merely brushed him aside, still following the one individual it had chosen irrevocably.

Huddled in silent horror, the three great bees saw it close with the captain, who buzzed shrilly in abysmal fear as jointed metal clamps gripped his chitinous body. At the last moment his own sting, ordinarily never used except for rare duels with his peers and ritual suicide on failing the Queen, flashed into sight as custom went by the boards under the urge for self preservation. The keen, amber lance, dripping yellow venom, stabbed hard against the ruum, breaking off short even as the greenish syringe plunged home into the commander's thorax. Instantly the captain fell back, his shimmering wings limp, completely paralyzed. The glitter of his compound eyes faded to a mere gleam, and his palps gave a few pathetic wriggles.

Panic stricken, the others broke for the hatch, but Briz, suddenly aware of his command responsibility, flung them back.

"Wait!" he panted. "Set the auto-pilot for home. Maybe we can keep out of its way—"

The quick minded technician saw his point, plunged past Sergeant Srt, and leaped to the controls. It took only a moment to set the computer for their home planet, and maximum acceleration. Then the ruum, through composing its specimen's limbs in a more orderly way, poked a curious rod in their direction. Buzzing, the three fled, and its velocity mounting rapidly, the scout raced for home.

A council of desperation was held immediately, at the farthest end of the ship, since the survivors expected prompt pursuit. There, surrounded by a battery of heavy armament, the three disconsolate bees took stock of their strange predicament. After years of undisputed conquests, they were psychologically unprepared to deal with the invincible sphere.

"This is no place to start a colony," the lieutenant said with grim humor. "It's very lucky we followed the book and avoided those cities. If isolated individuals have such remarkable equipment, just think of their police and armies. We'd have been destroyed in seconds."

"You can't believe that, sir," the sergeant said dully. "We are the highest form of life there is."

"Tell that to the creature inside the sphere," Briz replied in a bitter voice. "Do you suppose, Wrzs, that this heavy ray generator, if we dismounted it to turn inward, could blast the thing? After all, it has destroyed other spaceships in a flash."

31

"Frankly, sir, I doubt it. The hand ray didn't get past the surface dust. There isn't that much difference, basically."

"I'm afraid you're right," the officer agreed gloomily. "But what then?"

Sergeant Srt spoke up, briskly confident. "If we could lure it into the combustion chamber …"

"Even if that worked," the lieutenant objected, "we might ruin the ship's drive. We can't risk that so far from home. It's not a matter of our lives, but of warning our Queen about this terrible race."

At the mention of the great, immobile, egg-laying bulk, the life and Goddess of their kind, the three bowed their heads.

"It's a pity we didn't get a look at the x-ray pictures," the technician said. Then he added, with more animation: "Sir, have you noticed—it hasn't left the control room. I don't think it's coming after us at all. We could try to make terms."

"Terms!" The officer was outraged. "With the murderer of our noble captain?"

"I think he means, sir," the sergeant explained, "just until we get back. After that—" He paused, meaningly.

"Well," Briz admitted, without marked enthusiasm, "it might be worth a try." Then, almost automatically: "Sergeant, take over!"

His subordinate, vainly trying to conceal his chagrin at the dangerous assignment, collected, in reproachful silence, signal lamps, electronic communicators, and even old fashioned buzz-boxes. Saluting ostentatiously, he listened at the door, opened it with great reluctance, and slipped out. The officer and the technician waited tensely. Finally, when some thirty minutes had passed, the sergeant returned, the strained look gone from his faceted eyes.

"No luck, sir," he reported. "It's just resting there by the—by Captain Zril. It ignored all attempts at communication, but didn't attack me. Just put out a few rods and lenses. I think it's terrified at being out in space. You know, it may have acted the way it did out of sheer panic. Anyhow, we can use the control room now. I saw the x-ray pictures, too."

"What's inside the vehicle?" the lieutenant demanded.

"No use, sir—the shell is so dense that we never got through the surface. Maybe if we try again, with about ten hours' exposure at full power ..."

"Well, anyway we're headed for home, and the creature is bewildered and helpless so long as we don't scare it into fighting us again." He rubbed the edges of his wings together in satisfaction. "We'll notify them, the minute we're within range, to bring up our heaviest defense weapons. This damned thing inside the ball will regret killing our captain, I promise you. The second we land, it'll be immobilized with really big beams, and then—" He paused, eyes glittering with feral anger. "I shall ask our great Queen to let *me* dissect it."

"Sir, I almost forgot," the sergeant said. "The Captain is still alive."

"Alive!"

"Yes, sir. His palps were trembling, and his eyes had some life spark. He's just paralyzed by that green liquid the sphere injected."

"But if you had the run of the control room, why didn't you carry Captain Zril out so we could treat him?"

"I tried, but it's no use. The minute I came near the Captain, the thing became agitated. I didn't dare. It won't let us touch him, that's plain."

"A hostage!" the officer exclaimed. "But then why didn't it communicate? What does it want? I don't understand—" He stopped. It wasn't proper in the Service to display too much ignorance before one's subordinates. Too bad about Zril, but they were helpless. It was more important to get back with this vital information about a— possibly—superior race. Back home, after taking care of the lifeform inside the sphere, they'd get the commander to a hospital, where no doubt he could be saved. Whether his official reputation could survive the disgrace was another matter.

But Lieutenant Briz didn't allow for the fanatic loyalty of the technician. That night, when the other two bees were asleep, Wrzs sneaked out, and went to the control room. There, his gallant but ill-advised attempt to rescue the captain set in train a fateful sequence of events.

It was the ruum's business to collect one typical specimen within the weight limits set by the long dead captain of the *Ilkor*. There was no reason for the efficient robot to bother the remaining bees. Nor had it any setting requiring it to return to the Earth. So far as it knew, it was still on the ground, and within its assigned radius of operations, since only its own rolling motion registered as distance traveled on the intricate computers inside.

One other thing was within its capabilities, and it amounted to a solemn duty: a ruum was built to protect its specimens from injury and molestation. For millions of years it had successfully guarded its collection in the Rockies. The green liquid made the paralyzed bodies, still alive, unpalatable to other predators, and many a grizzly had died while attempting an easy meal in the ruum's butcher shop.

It follows that when Technician Wrzs crept into the control room and foolishly tried to drag out Captain Zril, the great sphere rolled into prompt action, driving the bee away with an overwhelming display of force. Mercifully indifferent, aside from its mission, the robot did not kill the intruder, but—and this is significant—it made the control room off limits from then on.

The dutiful Wrzs confessed his mistake to the lieutenant, who promised him a speedy court martial at home, but the damage was done. A few attempts soon convinced the bees that it was no longer possible to reach the controls; the ruum harried them out in seconds. There was no solution; the robot held the nerve center of the ship, and the scout, at an acceleration almost beyond conception, was hurtling with perfect accuracy for the main spaceport of their home planet.

During that terrible twenty-four hour approach period, they made repeated attempts to reach the controls, only to be met at the door by the vigilant ruum, more concerned than ever for its first new specimen in many years.

When a mere six hours from home, the three bees realized that nothing could save them and their vital information, and feeling utterly disgraced in having failed the Queen, they made a final invocation, and loudly buzzing Her praises, stung themselves honorably to death.

At the last moment the emergency controls managed to stop any further acceleration, but even so, when the ship plunged into the spaceport, too fast for the most sensitive detectors to flash any warning, it destroyed that installation utterly, leaving a glowing crater five miles across.

There was nothing alive around to see a spherical object roll casually out of the seething pit, flicker a few instruments towards the Royal Capitol, just visible over the horizon, and move at a relentless five miles an hour in the direction of the Imperial Palace.

After a million years of activity, even the perfect robot must show some signs of wear; and a minor defect may occur even with the product of a peerless technology. It was most unfortunate for the bee-people and their plans of conquest that in the almost inconceivable force of the ship's impact, the ruum's basic setting was jarred from a mere 160 pounds to its maximum of 3,500.

For the Queen Bee, the Source of All, and Only Mother of the Race, busily laying eggs in the Imperial Palace twenty miles away, weighed exactly 3,500 pounds.

Turning Point

It was that unhappy time when Earth was ruled by the Empire of the Rats. From pole to pole, the word of the Rat Emperor was law, neither to be questioned nor evaded by any rodent nor by any man.

Throughout man's early history, the rat had been one of his chief rivals for dominance, along with the insects. Lacking both the intelligence of such near-men as the higher apes, and the blind, irresistible fertility of the insects, the rats began with a fair share of the two advantages. Their forepaws were not as dexterous as a monkey's fingers, but distinctly better than hoofs or talons; and their litters, while no match for aphid eggs, were large and viable all over the globe.

Originally small in size—from an inch or two in the case of mice, to a foot or more in some tropical species of cane rats, and even larger in related species, like the capybara—the rats had profited from man's own belligerence and ruthlessness. And his perverted science. The Atomic War that began in 2092 exterminated roughly ninety per cent of all life on Earth. Humanity was back to its primitive beginnings, with small, scattered, barbaric tribes surviving in odd corners of the globe. The insects came out best, numerically, but hadn't the genetic stuff to take full advantage of their temporary dominance. The rats, decimated, but much more resistant to hard radiation than man, were favored by nature, inscrutable and capricious as ever in her workings.

The rodents mutated to an unusual degree, becoming not only much bigger, but greatly improved mentally, with a new power of abstraction. When some rat-genius was able to note and understand the connection between two burrows and the idea of a pair, the handwriting was on the wall for anybody to read; but there were few prophets among the remnants of human civilization to interpret the omens.

With their frequent litters, and generations that came and went in hundreds before a man grew old, the rats maintained their vital lead. Before long they were reading, and using, man's own written records, a fair proportion of which had survived the war. Those few communities that still had retained technical competence, fought hard, using rifles, poison, flame, and gas; but were overwhelmed by the enemy, which was willing to die in his thousands to kill or capture a single human.

There was a great deal of irony in the resulting situation. The rats, because of their racial memories of man, were oddly ambivalent towards the species. On the other hand, they remembered, with fury, the traps, ferrets, and agonizing chemicals of the past. But they also recalled, in some queer emotional way, that no brown rat was ever happy living in the wilds away from man—and it was not merely a matter of food and shelter. The rats actually liked to have people around; and even now, when man was subordinate—a conquered race—the rats felt the same way.

Naturally, the humans had no such tolerance; they had always hated and feared rats; and that hadn't changed. An added irony could be found in the relatively merciful treatment afforded man by the Empire of the Rats. People were allowed to live in their own communities, provided the rats had full access to them at all times. A close watch was kept to see that no dangerous weapons were invented or rebuilt; and above all, reproduction was sternly controlled—the human population was kept absolutely and irrevocably fixed at ten thousand. The rats knew very well that if man was ever allowed unchecked breeding, he would, in his fierceness and intelligence, regain the ascendancy just lost by the Atomic War.

Wise in their reading of history, the rats even had a safety valve for the release of social pressure—the sort built up by fanatical and ingenious malcontents: the Garrisons, Hitlers, Toussaints, and Ghandis of the time. Anybody who so desired, was permitted to emigrate beyond the control of the Emperor. There was one place on Earth—a region of South America—where no rat could survive. In those thousands of square miles of steaming jungle, a virus disease had developed that was quickly fatal to rats, but had no effect on man. It is possible that with enough time and trouble—and the doubtful help of human scientists, who were often necessary to rat-technology, and so coddled at need—the rats could have solved the problem, and made the region habitable. But it wasn't worth the effort; there was still plenty of space, since the Earth was starting again from scratch, so to speak.

Their tolerance was remarkable. Instead of killing such malcontents, as many human tyrants have done, and unwisely, as it turned out, the rats allowed them to emigrate to the Amazon. But the rodents were not stupid. Anybody who wished to leave had to submit to sterilization; there would be no hidden population explosion in the jungle. Unable to breed, the colony of humans was not a danger to the Empire. Sterilization was accomplished by x-rays and drugs, and great care was taken to make sure it was irreversible by surgery; it was not just a matter of cutting cords in the male, but a thorough operation just short of emasculation, done, of course, in a hospital under the best, most painless, and aseptic conditions. With a woman, the ovaries were removed. A human surgeon could be used, under the supervision of a rat, equally well qualified, but slightly less dexterous, as both species knew.

The mutated rats, it should be pointed out, were still not as big as men, but stood about four feet tall on their hindpaws, the front ones having become very much like hands, but not quite as flexible, lacking a completely opposable thumb. Communication between the two species, strangely, was in English plus an admixture of other human languages. The rats, after all, had learned reading and writing from documents, books, records, and films of their ancient enemy. A rat's voice was still squeaky, but no less lucid than that of a hoarse and excited girl soprano, for example; and people soon learned to catch every nuance of the conversation—or orders.

The rat species had always been community centered; the rodents liked to live together, and were quick to respond to the calls of any member of the group that was in trouble. So it was natural for the mutants to live in huge rat-cities, built to their own specifications, and above ground, but more than faintly mirroring human areas long since destroyed by nuclear fire.

Unknown to the rats—otherwise it could not have happened—the turning point came on August 20, 2167. A young scientist and his wife had applied for an emigration permit. The rats did not like to see trained humans leave their control, but the Emperor's policy was fixed; he and his council believed, as students of history, that it was best to allow malcontents to go away from the community—the farther the better—as long as they were made harmless first.

The Rat-Commissioner of Emigration, who issued the final papers, was a grey-brown rodent slightly smaller than the average, but with very keen, beady eyes, too undersized for his great forehead. His stiff, white whiskers were neatly trimmed. He wore no clothes, not belonging to that tiny, antisocial group of his kind that affected human garb, and spoke of the barbarity of nakedness. There were armed guards, but more as matter of honor and prestige than need. Mankind had no power weapons, and none could be smuggled into the South American colony: there were too many rats on guard, and they were equipped with keener senses than man, able to see, smell, and whisker-feel in the worst light. Besides, in their immense bureaucracy, patterned after man's own, there were records of everybody's movements, papers to be filled out, and serial numbers for every artifact that might be turned against the Empire. If so much as an ancient revolver was moved from one house to another, the fact was instantly known and evaluated by a computer. Tight control, the rats knew, was their only chance—short of exterminating man—to stay on top. It is to their credit that they never seriously considered genocide.

"Walter Nolan," the Commissioner squeaked. "And wife, Gloria, born Gloria Bandini. Why do you want to leave, Mr. Nolan?"

"It's all down there," was the cold reply. "Why make me repeat it?"

"It says you can't breathe," the rat said. "Have we been so hard on you? You went to a good university; became a fine engineer. We have given you many advantages in pay and privileges."

"I want to be free," Nolan said stubbornly. "You wouldn't understand that."

"I'm afraid not," the Commissioner said, with a note of genuine regret in his voice. His beady eyes twinkled. "You see, when my people were slaves—or at least, not free—we didn't have the intelligence, consciousness, or civilization to know it. We died from poison, terriers, gas, and such horrors as dumb animals, without comprehension."

"I make no excuses," the man said. "Rats—the primitive, early kind, if I have the facts straight—were a great menace to my species. They destroyed more food than they actually ate; they carried dangerous diseases; and even killed or injured children."

"As to that last," was the dry retort, "your slum landlords and thieving politicians were more to blame than my kind, who knew no better, being only insentient brutes at that stage of their evolution." He sighed. "However, I see your mind is made up. But let me point out that we know what many of you are hoping for. You think that once out of our control you can mount a successful revolt against the Empire. Now we understand that a group of intelligent and dedicated men—fanatics—can produce, in spite of our safeguards, a core army, with excellent weapons. But because you can't multiply, and emigration is to be kept at reasonable levels in addition, you can always be overwhelmed if you leave your own country—and it is your own; we never trespass."

"Because you can't, and live," Nolan pointed out.

"That's true; but we could find a suicide squad or two to penetrate the jungle and report before dying of the virus. But our controls make such a sacrifice pointless. Even with a new and potent weapon for each of you, a million rats with automatic arms, artillery, and even tanks, would crush you easily; that's obvious."

"But no planes," Nolan said.

"I admit that we rats have a racial horror of flight, perhaps because of hawks and owls; but neither can you make planes in the jungle villages—not now. If and when you do, a few hundred men can't pilot enough of them to destroy thousands of our communities. And there would be ample warnings; your borders are always watched, as you will learn."

He picked up the dossier. "The papers are in order. Your wife has had an ovariotomy, and you are completely sterile—or so it says. But," he added, looking at them keenly, "we never accept mere papers. I'll call the hospital and check with the surgical chief."

He pressed a lever on his intercom, and was soon through to the hospital listed on the form. After requesting a check, he listened to the squeaky sounds for some moments.

"I see," he said. "She aborted some days earlier. Then you operated. Yes, I understand." He turned off the intercom, and again faced the couple. "The surgeon tells me your wife had a miscarriage a day or two before coming for the required operation."

"If you must know," Nolan said in a hard voice, "she lost our baby because she so resented having one brought up a slave to rats. It was my idea to have it, anyhow. Now we're going away where if there are no babies, there is freedom from rats."

"All right," the Commissioner said. "Believe me, I'm sorry—about the baby." He stamped the essential passport, handed it to Nolan, and said: "You know the routine. You and your wife will be escorted to the boundary of the colony, and turned over to a man of your own future community. Good luck, and if you ever want to come back—"

"If I do," Nolan said grimly, "it won't be as a pliant subject of the Emperor, I assure you, but as an armed invader. I give you fair warning. You can search my baggage, and make me sterile, but nobody can ransack or neutralize this." He tapped his head.

The Commissioner gave him a grave and steady scrutiny for some seconds, his whiskers bristling. But when he spoke, his voice was level. "Goodbye, both of you," he said. "Next case, please."

Once outside the office, Gloria looked anxiously at the guards accompanying them to the bus, but they were well beyond earshot.

"Why so belligerent, for Heaven's sake?" she asked her husband. "Were you deliberately trying to make him angry? Did you see his whiskers? He could have canceled us out, you know; then where would we be?"

"I was scared stiff—that call to the hospital. I know they check, but for a minute, I thought he was on to us. So I tried to play the bitter, but planless, malcontent—a guy burned up, but with only generalities

41

to threaten. And it seemed to work—at least, he didn't go into the abortion."

"They don't care about that; I'm not carrying a baby; that's enough for them. And I can't have any more," she added, her voice quivering briefly. "And you—never to be a father."

Once past the borders of the free territory, and heading for the largest community, deep in the jungle, called *Voltaire*, Nolan was quick to reassure their guide.

"It worked," he said, exultation in his voice. "They were completely fooled. Gloria—poor kid—has no ovaries; and me, I'm as sterile as any old mule; but our son is alive, and safe. Not in a little jar—that didn't work out; and anyway, they go through the luggage too thoroughly; even x-rays, which would be fatal. No, Doctor Soburu just implanted the fertile egg in my own peritoneum, where it will be quite all right for several days, at least. As soon as we reach *Voltaire*, one of your surgeons can put it back on the wall of Gloria's womb."

"Right," the guide said. "It should work. And if it does, you two are only the first. Others are coming soon; and even if the rats cut off all emigration later, we need only a few children—they won't be sterile! It took only Adam and Eve to give us 2,000,000,000 people, remember! We're on the way back."

At the Royal Palace, the Emperor of the Rats stirred uneasily in his sleep.

As well he might.

The Rescuer

It was by far the largest, most intricate machine ever built.

Its great complex of auxiliary components covered two square blocks, and extended hundreds of feet beneath the earth. There were fifty huge electronic computers at the heart of it. They had to be capable of solving up to thirty thousand simultaneous partial differential equations in as many variables in any particular millisecond. The energy which the machine required to operate successfully on a mass of M pounds was given by a familiar formula: $E=MK^2$. The K was not, as in Einstein's equation, the velocity of light; but it was large enough so that only one type of power could be used: the thermonuclear reaction called hydrogen fusion.

Designing the machine and developing the theory of its operation had taken thirty years; building it, another ten. It had cost three billion dollars, an amount to be amortized over roughly one hundred years, and supplied by fifteen countries.

Like the atomic bomb, the machine could not be tested piecemeal; only the final, complete assembly would be able to settle the question of success or failure. So far, no such trial of its capabilities had been made. When the time came, a one-milligram sample of pure platinum would be used.

It was the largest, most intricate, expensive, fascinating, and dangerous machine ever built. And two men were about to destroy it. They would have to release a large amount of thermonuclear energy in order to wreck the machine. It was the only way in the circumstances.

It was a heartbreaking decision to have to make. Perhaps they should have contacted higher authorities in Washington, since the machine, although quite international in scope, was located in

California; but that was too dangerous with time so short. Bureaucratic timidity might very well cause a fatal delay. So, knowing the consequences to them, the two scientists did what they believed had to be done. The machine, together with several blocks of supporting equipment, including the irreplaceable computers, was vaporized. They escaped in a fast air car.

PRELIMINARY HEARING—A TRANSCRIPT
THE UNITED STATES versus DR. CARNOT
THE UNITED STATES versus DR. KENT
April 14, 2015
(Extract)

JUDGE CLARK: How did the man know the operation, when the machine had never even been tested?

DR. CARNOT: The theory had been widely discussed in many scientific papers—even popular magazines. And the man was a technician of sorts. Besides, it wasn't necessary to understand the theory; not more than forty or fifty men in this country could. He must have seen numerous pictures of the controls. The settings are simple; any engineer can use a vernier.

JUDGE CLARK: I think you'd better tell this court just what happened from the beginning. Your strange reticence has caused a great deal of speculation. You understand that if found guilty, you must be turned over to the U.N. Criminal Court for prosecution.

DR. CARNOT: Yes, Your Honor; I know that.

JUDGE CLARK: Very well. Go ahead.

DR. CARNOT: Dr. Kent and myself were the only ones in the area that night. It was a matter of chance that we decided to check some minor point about the bus bars. To our astonishment, when we arrived at the control room, the machine was in operation.

JUDGE CLARK: How did you know the machine was being used?

DR. CARNOT: In many ways; all the indicators were reacting; but primarily the mass-chamber itself, which had dislimned and assumed the appearance of a misty, rainbow-colored sphere.

JUDGE CLARK: I see. Go on.

DR. CARNOT: Dr. Kent and I were shocked beyond expression. We saw from the readings that the person, whoever he was, had entered for a really fantastic number of ergs—that is, energy. Far more than any of us would have dared to use for many months, if at all.

(At this point Senator King interposed a question.)

SENATOR KING: How did the fellow get into the area? What about the Security?

DR. CARNOT: As you know, the machine is international, and sponsored by the U.N. Since there is no longer any military rivalry among the members, the work is purely scientific, and no country can be excluded. Naturally, the complex is protected against crackpots; but this man worked on the project as a Class 5 technician, and must have known how to avoid the infrared and other warning systems.

JUDGE CLARK: We had better not confuse the issue with such digressions. How the man got in is no longer important. But your sudden knowledge of his background is, Dr. Carnot. In an earlier statement you claimed to have no information about his identity. How do you explain that?

DR. CARNOT: I had to lie.

JUDGE CLARK: Had to?

DR. CARNOT: Yes, Your Honor. All of that will become clear, I hope, later in my testimony. Right now, let me clarify our dilemma. The machine was definitely in operation, and had been for about eight minutes. We couldn't be certain that it would work—I mean to the extent of completing the job as programmed by the intruder; but the theory had been carefully investigated, and all the computations, which, as you know, took many years, checked out. It is a peculiarity of the machine, related to the solution of thousands of the most complicated differential equations, that there can be neither a cessation nor a reversal of its operation without grave danger to the entire state—perhaps even a larger area. The combination of vast energies and the warping of space-time that would result, according to theory, might vaporize hundreds of square miles. For this reason, and others, our plans had not gone beyond trying masses less than one gram.

JUDGE CLARK: Let me understand your point. It was impossible merely to shut off the machine? Stop the power?

DR. CARNOT: If the theory is sound, yes. I can only suggest the analogy of breaking an electrical circuit involving millions of amperes—the current jumps the gap, forming an arc that is very difficult to stop. Well, in this case, it was not merely millions of amps, but energies comparable only to those emitted by a large mass of the sun itself. In short, the only way to prevent completion of this particular operation was to bleed off enough of that energy to destroy most of the complex. That, at least, would save the populated areas. Remember, we had only about twelve minutes in which to choose a course of action.

JUDGE CLARK: But you weren't even sure the machine would work; that is, that the man would really survive. Yet you deliberately wiped out a three billion dollar project.

DR. CARNOT: We simply couldn't risk it, Your Honor. If the man did survive, and succeeded in his mission, the dangers were almost inconceivable. Even philosophically they are more than the human mind can grasp.

JUDGE CLARK: But neither of you has been willing so far to explain that point. This court is still completely in the dark. Who was the man, and what did he attempt to do?

DR. CARNOT: Up to now, we weren't ready to speak. But if you will clear the court except for yourself, the President, and a few high, responsible officials, I'll try to satisfy this tribunal. The fact is, as you will see, that a large part of the public, in this country, at least, might approve of what that man tried to do. It may not be possible to convince laymen—people not used to the abstractions of philosophy or science—of the great risk involved. I can only hope that this court will appreciate the implications. I should add that Dr. Kent and myself have seriously considered refusing any further information, but merely pleading guilty to willful destruction of the machine. As it is, if you decide to release us to the U.N. for criminal proceedings, we still might have to do just that—which means your records would have to be suppressed. Our only reason for testifying is not to save our own lives, but the hope that we can contribute to the design of a new machine. And to better understanding of the problems involved in the operation. Among the public, that is.

JUDGE CLARK: I must take your attitude seriously; that is very plain. Do you persist in maintaining that this room should be cleared, and all broadcasting suspended? Press, distinguished scientists, senator—all these are not qualified to hear the testimony?

DR. CARNOT: I only mean that the fewer who hear me, the fewer mouths to be guarded. And I'm sure this court will feel the same way when all my evidence is in.

JUDGE CLARK: Very well, then. The bailiffs will clear the room, except for the President, the National Security Council, and the Chairman of the Research Committee of the Congress. All electronic equipment will be disconnected; a complete spy curtain will be put on this room. Court will adjourn for two hours, reconvening at 1500.

PRELIMINARY HEARING
(Continued)

JUDGE CLARK: We are ready to hear your testimony now, Dr. Carnot.

DR. CARNOT: Do I have Your Honor's absolute assurance that nobody outside this room can hear us?

JUDGE CLARK: You do. The spy curtain, which your own colleagues in science claim bars all wavelengths, is on at full strength.

DR. CARNOT: If I seem too cautious, there is a reason, as you will see.

JUDGE CLARK: I certainly hope so. Now, will you please give the real point of this testimony? What was the man—and incidentally, has any identification come in on him yet? No? Well, what was he doing that seems to have scared you so?

DR. CARNOT: His name doesn't matter; it was on the note he left.

JUDGE CLARK: What note? Nothing was said about a note. Here this court has been trying to identify the man, and all the time—

DR. CARNOT: I'm sorry, Your Honor; that is part of the testimony we thought had better be withheld until now. The man did leave a note, explaining just what he meant to do with the time machine.

JUDGE CLARK: And what was that?

DR. CARNOT: He had set the dial for a two thousand year trip into the past. That accounted for the vast amount of energy required. You see, it varies not only with the mass transported, but the time as well.

JUDGE CLARK: Two thousand years!

DR. CARNOT: That's right, Your Honor. In itself, that's bad enough. It is one thing to send a small mass or a sterile insect back in time; even then, there are dangers we can hardly predict. The present is intricately involved with the past—stems from it, in fact. It's like altering the origin of a river; a little change at the source can make a tremendous difference at the mouth. Even move it fifty miles away. Now a modern man in the world of two thousand years ago—frankly, Your Honor, we just don't know what that might do. It seems fantastic to believe that he could change the here-and-now, and yet the theory implies that this whole universe might change completely, or even vanish. Don't ask me where or how.

(At this point Professor Pirenian of the National Security Council broke in with a question.)

PIRENIAN: Why didn't you and Dr. Kent merely send another man to intercept this one? Yours, by the machine, could obviously set the dials to get there first, thus snatching the first one back before he could do any harm.

DR. CARNOT: We thought of that, even in the few minutes we had. But suppose before we could cut in ahead of him that this world vanished? Believe me, the paradoxes are maddening; no amount of mathematical wrangling can settle them; only experiment. We couldn't chance it; that's all.

PIRENIAN: You're right, of course. Maybe we should be glad, gentlemen, that Dr. Carnot—and Dr. Kent—were there instead of the rest of us!

DR. CARNOT: You still don't know the real danger. What I've said so far applies to an impulsive, random trip to the distant past, where the man had no specific intentions. But Michael Nauss did have a particular plan—a wild, crazy, and yet, in a way, magnificent conception. One that the public, or much of it, might foolishly support without realizing the consequences. I speak of this country, and people in Europe; not in Asia, for the most part. And he had set the vernier with perfect precision, which made his plan even more feasible.

JUDGE CLARK: What was he going to do?

DR. CARNOT: According to his note, this man had taken with him a repeating rifle and five thousand rounds of exploding ammunition. His intention was nothing less than to arrive at Golgotha in time to rescue Jesus Christ from the Roman soldiers. In short, to prevent the Crucifixion. And with a modern rifle, who can say he wouldn't succeed? And then what? Then what? The implications are staggering. Disregarding the Christian dogma, which asserts Jesus *had* to die for our sins, what of the effect on the future, the entire stream of history, secular as well as religious. Maybe Jesus Himself would have prevented this madman from saving Him—but who can be sure? Yet, if you ask the man in the street, now, in this year 2015: "Shall we save Jesus Christ from the cross?"—what would he answer? Whose side would he take? Ours, or Michael Nauss'? That is why Dr. Kent and I destroyed the machine; and why we face this court now. We believe the proceedings should not be released. The decision is yours. We made ours that night.

Problem Child

If relief from pain can be found in absorbing mental work, then the mathematician is among the most fortunate of men. In every direction, beyond the well-cultivated plains of basic analysis, lie the unscaled peaks of the great problems, attacked, some of them for generations, and always without success. And surrounding them, or lying over the horizon, out of sight, whole new empires awaiting their inevitable conquerors.

Professor Kadar was like a man within sight of Paradise, but unable to find a path through the impassable terrain that blocked his way. He had patiently tried hundreds, all promising, only to be confronted, at the last moment, by the same yawning chasm that indicated No Highway.

Now it had checked him again. He dropped the pen, sighed, and put his head in his hands. There was a small, sucking sound, and the professor looked up. Briefly, he had forgot; that was one virtue of the thorny analysis that sprawled over a ream of yellow second sheets.

How long had the child been there? He came and went so silently these days. Perched on the tall chrome bar stool, so incongruous a seat for a three-year-old, he slumped like a Buddha across from his father. And always with that same inward look. The wizened face, still wearing that aged-in-the-womb expression of the newborn infant, seemed vaguely Oriental to Kadar today. Not a Mongolian idiot, definitely, the clinical psychologist had assured him. Just retarded.

The professor's eyes, deep socketed and melancholy, met Paul's, which had, he felt, an unmistakable slant. He was conscious, more strongly than ever, of his son's sweetness and placidity. Odd that they should be so characteristic of the mentally retarded child. As if nature desired to compensate the cheated parents. Not that it was ever compensation enough. And in this case, when he remembered—could he really forget, even for a moment, even when that path to Paradise seemed open?—that Eleanor had died to birth this little vegetable, it was no comfort at all.

The slanting eyes, small and dark, turned inward again. Oriental or gypsy? Many Hungarians had Romany blood. Or was the doctor—all those experts he had consulted—wrong, and Paul Mongoloid?

Names, Kadar reflected bitterly. What did they mean? In mathematics, you called something a ring, a cycle, an ideal. What you named it was unimportant; all that mattered was its place in the structure—never things, but the relations among them; those were what counted. What was Paul's relation to the world, now and in the future?

For the present, he was only a baby; in many ways, less than a baby. Mrs. Merrit was a kind, motherly woman; not intelligent; not educated; but warm. Paul obviously liked her, if he responded to anybody, which was doubtful. His normal expression, in an adult, often suggested profound boredom.

The professor thought about the tests—the endless, expensive tests. Colored doodads, blocks, strings, geometric forms to be matched—and the brisk, young men and women who presided over the rituals. Paul had confounded all of them; Kadar felt a perverse glow of satisfaction at the thought. The boy didn't make mistakes; instead, he simply refused to cooperate. Of course, it was nothing to rejoice over. Apathy meant even more severe brain damage, the doctors seemed to think. And Paul's electroencephalographs certainly were abnormal, suggesting those of an advanced epileptic.

The child nibbled at his lips again, making that tiny murmur in his throat. The eyes turned outward briefly, met Kadar's somber gaze, then Paul slipped clumsily from the high stool and padded from the room, moving with the rather unbalanced gait of a sedentary elder.

Off for some lunch, Kadar thought. Why didn't Mrs. Merrit call the boy, instead of letting him set his own schedule? My fault, he told himself immediately. I'm letting her raise him, while I try to forget Eleanor—yes, and him, too—in my work. On the other hand, why impose disciplines on a child who never rebels? The sweet placidity of Paul was reflected in his childish routines. He ate whatever was given him—but only if hungry. He never cried; always lay quietly in bed when put there; and seldom got out until Mrs. Merrit came for him in the morning, although she mentioned occasionally, with some wonder, that he often was awake, stretched out under smooth bedclothes, with his eyes wide open.

Aside from that, his only quirk was the tall stool. At the age of two, he had already shown his preference for the flashy thing, climbing it to overlook Mrs. Merrit at her chores in kitchen and dining room.

Then, after the professor, acting on impulse, put the stool in his study, across from the big desk where he worked, Paul had come to prefer that location. Every day, for at least three hours, while Kadar scribbled away, the child sat there, sometimes apparently fascinated by the motion and hiss of the pen on paper, but more commonly with his eyes blank and unfocused.

Mrs. Merrit, naturally, thought this scandalous and unhealthy. For many weeks she tried to interest the child in a variety of toys, but without success. What the trained psychologists had been unable to accomplish, Kadar thought wryly, was not for a woman like his housekeeper to bring about between cooking and floor mopping.

Even retarded children may be good artists. But when given crayons and big sheets of paper, Paul had made a few tentative dabs, very awkwardly, and lost interest.

The boy must at least get some exercise, Mrs. Merrit insisted, so the professor bought a jungle gym, and, to his surprise, Paul condescended to scramble about in the thing for half an hour now and then. But Kadar suspected it was that same urge to attain purely physical elevation—did the child seek a height equivalent to that of the adults around him? Was that the only break in his apathy?

Paul came back to the study, and approached the stool.

"Come here, son," the professor said, moved to try establishing a relationship that always eluded him.

Meekly, in silence, Paul padded over. Kadar looked into the slanted eyes, searching for some kind of warmth. There were undoubtedly little lights inside, but they conveyed nothing to his understanding. He put one hand on the boy's silky hair, ruffling it, and Paul stepped back—not alarmed, but somehow rejecting the act. The professor felt a sudden urge to hug him, but quelled it, he couldn't have said just why. Paul went back to the stool, scrambled up in his queerly uncoordinated way, and sat there, lumpishly, his eyes again turned inward.

It came to Kadar, then, that Eleanor had sometimes worn such a look: an expression of deep self-communion. And yet—and yet— Uncle Janos had also looked that way often—Crazy Janos, who bungled everything he tried. Come to think of it, didn't Janos have an Oriental cast of features, too? It was all so far back, and in Hungary; Kadar couldn't remember. Besides, Janos died while his nephew was still a child.

The professor reached for a fresh sheet of paper, and began again, searching for the high road to Paradise. Fifty pages of the most advanced research—a new field of mathematics; a place beside Gauss, Abel, and Galois—hung on his finding that path. If a certain sequence converged to an irrational number, the key theorem and all that it implied was valid. And still the proof eluded him. Enough; enough; no more today; his head was on fire. Return with a fresh mind, like Poincaré and the Fuchsian Functions; that was the only hope, now. But he knew it wouldn't solve anything. Only a fresh approach, something revolutionary, could smash through the iron wall.

Swaying a little, almost like Paul in his gait, Kadar left the room. He mixed a stiff Martini, drank it slowly, and felt some of the tension go out of his muscles. Mrs. Merrit hastily made him a hot snack; she was resigned to his behavior, and knew better than to try changing it.

"Tell me," he asked her, "has Paul ever tried to say anything yet? Anything at all?"

"No," she said, her eyes full of sympathy. "Just little noises in his throat. But he understands; I'm sure he understands. You know how good he is about doing what we tell him."

"I know," Kadar said darkly. "That's hardly normal, either. No mischief; no rebellion; nothing. A vegetable—sweet, insipid; like a spoiled melon."

And he thought of Eleanor—vital, alert, bubbling; beauty without slickness or affectation; warmth without sentimentality. This was the child not of Eleanor and himself, but Crazy Janos: that was a typical joke of heredity—genes and DNA and Janos ending in Paul Kadar, whose father had five paragraphs in "American Men of Science."

He left most of the lunch untouched, and went back to the study. I won't work, he told himself; but maybe just glance over the equations again. Let my mind refresh itself; no use to keep prodding it. Deep inside his brain a tiny alarm bell was ringing. What if the theorem is false? What then? Fifty pages of meaningless squiggles: a magnificent structure with no foundation.

He entered the study, and walked to the desk. The top sheet lay there, mocking him—but what was this? The last equation was crossed out, and above it there was a long line of pencil marks. Almost like mathematical symbols, but not—by God, upside down!

Bewildered, he reversed the sheet. For a moment the writing still seemed without content, then Kadar felt his heart contract like a clenched fist. A new integral transform—powerful, elegant, and startlingly original. It would crack the tough kernel of the problem as lightning shatters an oak.

He looked up, wild-eyed. Paul met his gaze squarely. The slender throat was working; the lips moved.

"Like that ... it has to be like that. Other way ... the pattern is ugly," the boy mumbled, his voice a queer, high pitched stammer, as if he had to claw the words out of a diaphragm never before used.

Kadar, still uncomprehending, stared at the writing again. Upside down—because that's the way Paul, on his high perch, always saw the symbols. Their validity didn't depend on how they were written, of course.

An illiterate might conceivably, while listing words, write a simple declarative sentence. With luck, he might even hit upon a compound one, perfectly grammatical. But what were the odds against his writing immortal poetry, like: "Rough winds do shake the darling buds of May"?

Kadar looked at Paul again. The boy didn't need blocks or crayons because his mind saw every concept with perfect and immediate clarity. Just sitting on the high stool, he had absorbed a complete mathematical education from Kadar's work. Before that, he had overlooked Mrs. Merrit, but found nothing to stir his intellect. As for speaking, no doubt that, like his gait, was a matter of physique, and relatively unimportant to such a mind.

The professor felt a great surge of joy; yet, in a moment, it was tempered with sorrow. Paul was a monster, but a superior one. He was probably above—or beyond—love in the human sense. But their minds could commune, and maybe that was the best communion of all.

The Topper

If I hadn't been at the meeting myself, nobody, not even a committee composed of Albert Schweitzer, Bernard Baruch, and Winston Churchill, could have sold me the story of what happened.

Almost every Friday, our chief engineer on the project, Dr. Corman, held a briefing session. He's a first rate man, one of the best Cal Tech ever turned out, so we were glad to listen. All except Nils Larsen, that is. Corman is his boss, too, but Larsen hates to admit it. His specialty is miniaturization, and according to rumor, inscribing the Lord's Prayer on the head of a pin would be too simple for him; he would prefer to write "Gone With the Wind" there, instead.

But the queerest thing is that the two men can't find enough to fight about in engineering; they have to be amateur biologists for that. Corman has always maintained that some other form of intelligent life, besides man, was bound to turn up, either by mutation here on Earth, or on a neighboring planet. Larsen thought this was crazy; maybe he had some religious bias against the idea, or more likely he felt that way because opposition to the chief engineer was the spice of existence to him.

Ordinarily Dr. Corman would never have dreamed of using his Friday briefing period for anything else, but last night we knew something was up that had no connection with the Loki rocket.

There was the Chief with a powerful overhead projector, and on it a great, glass-topped box, thick bottomed and sturdy. A few of us, before the meeting got going, tried to come on stage for a peek, but Corman scowled us away. Clearly, he had planned a surprise, and didn't want anybody in the know ahead of time.

56

When everybody had arrived, and all were seated, with Nils Larsen right in the front row, as usual, Corman came up to the lectern. He's a big man, well over six feet, and broad in proportion, but oddly enough, his voice is a sort of shaky soprano. Larsen, small and chunky, sounds like a bullfrog by comparison.

"Gentlemen," Corman squeaked, sticking out his rocklike chin, "I know you will forgive me if I use this time for something other than the project. An event so startling and incredible has occurred that nothing else has any importance compared to it." He paused for a moment, fixing members of the first row with his glacial blue eyes. "I have discovered an intelligent form of life, right here in this community—in fact, in my own house."

"It can't be his wife," Jerry Noble muttered to me. "Her waist measurement exceeds her I.Q."

"Here in this box," Corman went on, glaring at Jerry, "are the first specimens of non-human, intelligent life. I must infer that as you have often heard me tell Larsen, they are mutants created almost certainly by the unusually high level of radiation from the proving ground."

I stole a glance at Nils; his face was twitching, as if he fought to suppress a grin.

Meanwhile a murmur of wonder had swept the group. They thought very highly of Corman's engineering skills; he was tops at theory as well as practice; the kind of man who could use matrix algebra or machine tools with equal facility. But this talk about a really astonishing discovery in another field had them puzzled.

The hum of conversation grew louder, and Corman raised a hand. When the audience was quiet again, he said: "I'm trying to prepare you for this gradually; otherwise it could be quite a shock. You see, the intelligent animals are—at least in appearance—very much like ordinary roaches." Here Larsen sputtered uncontrollably, his shoulders shaking. Corman gave him a single cryptic glance, then went on. "I found them in my own kitchen; you can imagine my amazement on seeing that they actually wore clothes of a sort—boots and garments." The hard-bitten group of engineers, mathematicians, and physicists gasped audibly at this. Larsen's neck was purple; he continued to shake.

"Before going on, let me show you," Corman said calmly. He switched on the projector, and dimmed the lights. Quickly he brought the contents of the glass-topped box into sharp focus on the screen.

This time you could almost hear all the eyeballs click to attention. It was the damnedest thing to see about a hundred large roaches, the German kind sometimes called croton bugs, rushing around in there, with each one wearing six little black boots and a brightly colored Indian type blanket fastened across its black, shiny back.

"Just look, gentlemen," Corman cried triumphantly. "If the use of such clothing doesn't prove their intelligence, I don't know what could. You have often heard me argue this point with Larsen; now you can judge who is right."

Instantly Nils was on his feet.

"Do you seriously maintain, Dr. Corman, that those insects are intelligent—mutants who have learned the use of clothing?"

"Absolutely."

"Will you stake your professional reputation on that?" the smaller man croaked.

"Without hesitation."

"Mr. Kellog," Larsen said, turning to a man three rows away. "Do you remember the sealed letter I gave you last week? The one I asked you to bring tonight?"

"Yes," Kellog admitted. "I have it here."

"Has it ever been out of your hands in the interval?"

"No. I kept it on me, as you suggested."

"Will you open it now, and read the contents to this group?" Larsen asked him, his lips twitching in a series of abortive grins.

"Of course," Kellog said.

He took a letter from his pocket, opened it, and read: "October 5th. Today I finished dressing nearly a hundred large roaches in tiny boots and bits of colored cloths. I used a syringe full of epoxy cement to make them stick. The roaches have complete freedom of movement. I intend to start planting them, twenty at a time, in Dr. Corman's house as a test of his gullibility." Kellog was smiling now. "It's signed by Larsen," he added.

"I think," Nils purred, "that the gullibility has been proved to the hilt. Your professional reputation I think you said, Dr. Corman," he said more maliciously.

Some of the people started to chuckle, and soon a ripple of mirth was spreading through the audience. But again Dr. Corman raised a hand for silence, and got it, so strong was his personality.

"Gentlemen," he said in a level voice several tones below his normal pitch. "This is a fantastic story Larsen is telling us." He looked squarely at the smirking Nils. "Do you remember how far up those boots extended?"

"Of course. Exactly two millimeters."

"In a moment you'll see that these are cockroach hip boots, almost five millimeters long."

"Absurd!" Larsen exclaimed.

"Did you put anything else on the roaches besides boots and blankets? Think carefully."

"I don't have to think—there was nothing else."

"The insects I found also wear little pouches. Inside them," he added meaningly, "is a set of most unusual tools."

"I don't believe it," Larsen snapped.

"Very well; look for yourself."

Once more he dimmed the lights and snapped on the projector. There was no doubt about it; each roach wore half a dozen boots extending well up its legs; and now we could see the tiny pouches on belts around their middles.

"It's a trick," Larsen yelled. "You did that yourself." Then his face fell. He was in a bind. Either way he lost. If he admitted Corman was capable of such miniaturization, his one superiority was lost. On the other hand, if the Chief hadn't done it, these were different, and possibly intelligent animals. But Corman wasn't through with his surprises.

"I had no idea Larsen was playing tricks," he said blandly, "but these can't be his roaches, because this bunch"—here he paused for effect—"can *communicate!*"

By this time we were all in a daze, but Nils looked really wild. Somehow his cute trick had been turned inside out trapping him within, like a weird Klein's Bottle.

"You're crazy!" he gulped.

"We'll see," Dr. Corman told him, his tone almost sinister.

He rapped on the box sharply; it was obviously a code message. I know Morse, and read it easily. He was ordering the roaches to give their mathematical demonstration. To the utter amazement of the whole pop-eyed group, the insects skidded and tumbled over each other to form a perfect right-angled triangle. Squares on the three sides, blackly shaded with shiny backs, demonstrated clearly the Pythagorean Theorem. Larsen dropped into his seat, his face the color of yogurt. The rest of us simply gaped.

Once more the chief engineer rapped on the glass. This time I heard him tell the roaches to say hello. Quickly, in the same frantic way, they spelled out with their bodies the phrase: "Hi, out there."

After that it was bedlam, with the whole group of men applauding, whistling, laughing, and stamping their feet. As for poor Larsen, he slumped in his chair, looking like a grape that's been stepped on by a rhino.

You may not want to give me credit, but I just didn't believe any of this. I've known Corman longer than the others; went to Cal Tech with him. Not many are aware of his sense of humor, which is far out, and seldom practiced. He's a virtuoso who performs only when a masterpiece is involved.

I was sure, naturally, that he'd amended the clothing of Larsen's roaches; it was the rest of the show—the "communication"—that baffled me. And yet it was so simple, as he demonstrated to the rest of us after Larsen went out, talking to himself and shaking his head. Simple, but ingenious, like all masterpieces.

Corman fed the roaches on starch paste with the finest iron filings mixed in. Electromagnets, carefully arranged and wired, did the rest. When that electric field formed a triangle, or a phrase, it really snatched those bewildered insects into line!

By today Larsen probably knows how he was taken. His idea was good, but no ordinary talent is a match for genius. Who remembers Wallace along with Darwin?

Controlled Experiment

"Objective evidence—laboratory controlled evidence—that's what it will take to convince *me*. And that's what the mystics can never produce!"

Nils Larsen glared at Dr. Corman as he delivered the challenge. Obviously, he was still smarting over the hoax of the intelligent roaches, and hoping to get back some of his own.

"Oh, I don't know," Corman said in his squeaky voice. He put a cigarette in his holder, undoubtedly aware of how the gesture annoyed Larsen, who preferred a rapid drumfire of interchanges in any argument.

"What do you mean, you don't know?" Nils rumbled, his thickset, stocky body seeming to contract like that of an angry cat. "You object to laboratory methods, to controlled, predictable experimentation?"

"Of course not." Corman lit the cigarette with great deliberation. "I mean that such evidence might be produced at any moment. Consider the reports of Soal, in England—"

Nils snorted, looking at the other scientists, and shaking his head.

"Why not go back to Sir Oliver Lodge, and the snapshots of fairies dancing in the garden!"

"As a matter of fact," Corman chirped, his voice as always a startling contrast to his big frame, "I've had some success myself of late. I'm not sure it's up to strict lab conditions …"

"I'll bet not!" Larsen boomed.

"… But Merritt and I have had remarkable success in telepathy."

"Telepathy? You and Merritt?" Nils' face was beet-red. "Another hoax, Corman?"

"Just because I made a harmless jest," Corman said, looking contrite, "you are becoming almost paranoid, Larsen. Relax, I have no intention of giving a demonstration, even though we've had almost unbelievable accuracy in transmission from my house to his."

It was impossible for Nils to refuse the bait. I looked at young Kahn, who sat next to me at the meeting, and we couldn't help grinning. Only six weeks since the cockroach fiasco, when Corman had seemed to make the insects, neatly clad in boots and harnesses, perform as if intelligent, to the extent of spelling out words with their bodies, and here was Nils ready for a rematch. Well, he was a top experimenter, and Corman would have to go some to fool him again.

"Just what did you transmit?" Larsen demanded. "Some of those vague diagrams, which when topologically equivalent are hailed as triumphs of telepathy? A thinks of a square, and B produces a lopsided rhomboid—lo, a fine datum!"

"No pictures," Corman said. "Just integers from one to ten. I've been able to think of any sequence of these, and Merritt, two hundred yards away, is able to write them down."

"Sure," Larsen snapped, "I could think of fifty ways the two houses might establish communication. Radio, black light; hell, Merritt could turn a good directional microphone towards your place, and pick up whispers."

"As I've said," Corman replied, puffing at his smoke, "you're getting quite paranoid. Why not ask Merritt?"

"He's your best friend; do I have to ask?"

"Why, Nils," Merritt said. "Don't you trust me, either?"

"With a million dollars, or even a new particle—but with tricks, never!"

Merritt patted his dog, a bright-eyed dachs, longer than a dull weekend. It wagged all over.

"Nip him," he told the animal, but it only wagged harder as Larsen walked over and gave it a pat.

"I trust Eulenspiegel here more than either of you." He stared at each man in turn, then added: "You want to play tricks, hey? This time you get fooled. If you can transmit the series of numbers *I* want, under *my* conditions, I buy dinner for the whole Committee. If not, you and Merritt pay. What do you say to that?"

"Depends on the conditions," Corman said, grinning at Merritt, who merely cocked his head quizzically.

"Right now," Larsen snapped. "Corman stays here, in this building, and Merritt goes two hundred yards away, into the parking lot. We can see from the window that he's there. And I search both of them; they could have miniature radios, the——"

The epithet was in Swedish, I think, and sounded highly insulting, but Corman just smiled.

"That's pretty strict," old Professor Martin said. "Especially for something as erratic as telepathy."

"Telepathy!" Larsen cried. "We all know better. When we get them like this, with no funny gadgets, they'll be lucky if any two of the numbers agree."

"It's all right with me," Corman said, to my surprise. I'd expected him to refuse. It had to be a trick, and how could they work it in such circumstances?

"You agree?" Larsen said, taken aback.

"With one reservation. I do have to be alone. Telepathy requires the most delicate and concentrated thought. Oh," he added, as Nils glared in suspicion, "you can put me in any room on this side of the place—the one that does not even face the parking lot."

Larsen reflected for a moment; he was considering every angle.

"First, I search," he said finally. And he did, with great care. There was no radio, no signal lamp, nothing that could have been used even with the two men in sight of each other. A similar examination of Merritt's pockets was equally negative.

"You can go to the parking lot," Larsen told Merritt, and he left, followed by Eulenspiegel, rejoicing at the prospect of a walk.

When Merritt was in the center of the lot faintly lighted by a big sodium lamp overhead, Nils ushered Corman into a small room. Most of the building, including our conference room, was between Merritt and Corman. The room had one tiny window, which was open a few inches. It was not big enough for even a dwarf to pass through. And eighteen of us watched the one door.

Going off by himself, Larsen wrote twelve numbers on a bit of paper, and showed it to Professor Martin, who made a copy which we all inspected.

"You can start computing their chances of matching these," Larsen grinned. "A dozen integers chosen at random, all less than eleven." He walked to the door of the room, slipped the paper under it, and said loudly: "Use your lighter to read these, and transmit them if you can. I'm looking forward to that dinner!"

There was a faint rustling sound inside as Corman picked up the paper. We listened, but heard nothing else. After almost ten minutes, when we were getting impatient, Corman came out.

"Merrit will be here with the results immediately," he announced, with perfect confidence, and Larsen gulped, his face going greenish.

"Merritt never left the lot," he said weakly. "I watched."

"That's right," Corman agreed. "He didn't have to. It's a very short distance for thought transmission." His eyes were twinkling.

A moment later Merritt returned. He tried to hand the paper he carried to Dr. Wallace, but Larsen snatched it himself. As he read the scribbled list of numbers, his jaw fell open. Old Martin took the slip from his hands, and compared it with our copy.

"Identical," he said laconically.

Larsen was squirming with annoyance.

"It's still a trick!" he roared. "Telepathy, hell!"

"If it's a trick," Wallace said, "let me in on it, Nils. You had everything going for you. No warning; no equipment—it beats me."

"I'll see you at dinner, gentlemen," Corman squeaked. He put one hand on Merritt's shoulder, and the two men left. Larsen was gobbling with fury; the rest of us were baffled, but amused. None of us had any increased confidence in telepathy.

Corman never did tell Larsen, but the other scientists got the real story, which to their credit, they kept to themselves for several weeks, until Nils almost burst.

It was another hoax, of course. Between Merritt, Corman—and Eulenspiegel. Corman's cigarette holder held a silent dog whistle, and the dach had been easily trained to bark softly at every blast. In the little room, a mere two hundred yards away, and with an open

65

window, all Corman had to do was play the number sequence on the whistle. In the parking lot, Merritt merely recorded the number of barks in each block of the message.

I'm not sure it will be safe to be around when Larsen gets the word.

The Formula

"Your mistake, Larsen, if you don't mind my saying so, is in letting Corman force the card you pick, so to speak—to let *him* set all the important conditions of the experiment."

The clear, slightly nasal voice, so full of assurance, was unmistakable. It belonged to Ken Lambert, a brash PhD, still in his early twenties, and a highly promising astronomer.

Sitting in the next booth with my coffee, I heard Larsen's rumbling denial.

"What do you mean? I put him in a separate room, on the farther side of the room. I had him searched. How could I think of a crazy trick like that dog whistle, silent to a man's ears, he signaled with?"

"I know; I know; it was clever of old Corman. But the thing is, if he tries another hoax, you must impose conditions *after* the bet is made—unexpected ones. Then he'll have to pay off without trying, or fail completely."

"He won't accept such a bet—why should he?"

"Because, clearly, he has an obsession about hoaxing you, and can't stop. He'll assume reasonable conditions, which he's already prepared for, and agree to the trial. Then you'll fix him for once."

I slipped quietly away. So Lambert was backing Larsen to catch Corman in his own trap. This would be worth watching. There was a conference due on Friday—the last of the year—which gave them four days to prepare. I debated mentally about warning Corman, but the negative won. It wouldn't be fair, and besides, Larsen deserved to get some of his own back if he could. I didn't even pass the word along, for fear Corman would be tipped off by somebody else.

On Friday, after the business of the meeting was over, the socializing began, with most of the wives coming in to join their husbands. Larsen and Lambert parked themselves a few feet away from Corman, watching him with a kind of anticipatory relish, like cannibals studying the latest missionary and estimating his weight on the hoof.

For almost an hour, nothing much happened. As usual, the men were talking shop, while their women, none too happily, formed little groups of their own.

Then, at seven fifteen, Warren Guild came in, announcing cheerfully: "Pretty warm out this evening, for May."

"Close to eighty-one, right now," Corman squeaked, turning his head for a brief, provocative glance towards Larsen.

"Been out to check?" Guild inquired.

"Don't have to," was the reply. "It's a sort of ESP thing with me. I can always tell what the temperature is outside, even from this air conditioned room."

I saw Lambert whisper something in Larsen's ear.

"Maybe the temperature is a simple linear function of the time," Larsen said coldly, "and so you figure out the equation."

"Think so?" Corman seemed amused. "The fact is, Nils, that the graph of temperature as a function of the time is not everywhere differentiable. Sometimes the temperature stays the same for several minutes; occasionally it even reverses itself."

Larsen hesitated. I could almost read his mind. Undoubtedly he was thinking that even if the relation was a complicated one, a man of Corman's ability might still have derived a good approximation formula for it. Lambert prompted him again.

"This is another one of your hoaxes," Larsen rumbled, with a kind of fierce eagerness. "Telling the temperature outside by ESP. No doubt you are even anxious to bet again."

"I hadn't thought about it," Corman said in a solemn voice. "It doesn't seem right to commercialize ESP."

Larsen's face turned purple; he was on the verge of sputtering. Only a few weeks earlier, Corman had demolished, in "Science," all the so called evidence for precognition based on cards.

"Still," Corman added, "there wouldn't be much harm in betting a dinner for the group again. Certainly, if I can't determine the outside temperature while sitting here in the room, I'll be happy to stand treat."

There was a dead silence, so that through the closed windows we could hear the shrill chirping of crickets in the shrubbery, and farther off, by the reservoir, the piping of tree frogs. Even the women were interested.

"I'll bet you," Larsen said grimly, "but this time I'll set the conditions. Otherwise, no deal."

"Up to a point, Nils. Up to a point. It can't be all one-sided. For example, temperature is obviously a continuous function of time, but the readings are not necessarily integral. And then there are microclimates—places only a few inches apart that have different temperatures. All I ask is that the thermometer be placed, say, two inches from the ground, roughly in the middle of the lawn, and that I be allowed an error of plus or minus two degrees. Aside from that, all conditions are yours."

Larsen caught Lambert's eye; the younger man nodded slightly; and Larsen said: "I accept." He rubbed his hands together, and announced: "First, you must strip down to your shorts—you'll wear Lambert's trench coat. No devices hid in cigarette holders this time, hey!"

"No objection," Corman squeaked. He went with Larsen and Lambert into an anteroom, and came out a few minutes later wearing Lambert's tan coat, much too short for him, so that his lean, hairy shanks were exposed. Some of the women giggled at the sight, but Corman was unperturbed.

Larsen now ostentatiously examined the old man's ears, and then blindfolded him. Not content with this, he glanced meaningly at the big electric clock on the wall, and seated Corman in an opposite corner, with his back to the dial.

"With ESP," he said, "you could tell the time without a clock. Besides, it won't matter what the clock says; when I ask for a reading, all you have to do is announce the temperature at that moment. Lambert and—Dr. Corby?—will you two get a thermometer, and put it

69

in the center of the lawn, about two inches up? Make a support from a stick and wire—yes?" The two men agreed, and left.

"You know, of course," Corman shrilled, "that none of these childish precautions affect ESP."

"Knock it off!" Larsen snapped. "*I* may believe in ESP, but you—never!"

"Ah, but it may be the unbeliever who has the power."

"That's right," Dr. Harris said, grinning. "He has a point, Larsen. According to experts, the espers are seldom aware of their talent, and may not even believe in it at first."

"We all know Corman's no esper," Larsen said. "This is just another trick, only it won't work. Want to pay up now, Corman?"

"On the contrary," the old man replied. "I'm anxious to demonstrate my talent immediately."

Oddly enough, it was Larsen who perspired visibly; his forehead was quite damp. And it was only seventy-eight in the room, and wouldn't have been that high, except for the women, who are always chilly.

Lambert returned.

"All set outside," he declared.

"Good," Larsen said. "This is how we'll do it. I'll ask Corman for a reading, then open the door, and call 'Mark One.' That's the signal for you and Dr. Corby to read the thermometer and record the temperature." He handed Lambert a clipboard. "When I call 'Mark Two,' do it again, and so on, for all ten entries. I think," he added turning towards Corman, "that such readings, at irregular, random intervals, should settle the matter."

"I agree," Corman said, and I thought his shoulders quivered slightly.

Larsen sent Lambert back out to Corby, checked Corman's blindfold, faced him more squarely into the blind corner of the room, and said: "Now, then—what's the temperature at this time?"

Even though there was no reason for it, the room became perfectly silent: a purely psychological reaction. I watched Corman closely, but he seemed relaxed. From my position far to one side, I noticed only one unusual thing. Normally, when sitting, he kept his hands in his pockets; but now, possibly because of having no pants under the coat, he seemed to have them clasped in his lap.

For a few seconds he didn't reply; then he said evenly: "Eighty-two degrees—Fahrenheit, of course."

Larsen whipped the door open, and yelled "Mark One!" Several of us in the room recorded Corman's estimate.

Larsen waited about eighteen minutes, and then demanded another reading.

"Still almost eighty-two," Corman said.

"Mark Two!" Larsen boomed to his assistants outside.

Normally, here on the edge of the desert, there is a rather rapid fall in temperature after sundown, so that nobody was surprised when later readings, irregularly spaced, were much lower. And once, because of some vagrant drift of warm air from the hot flats, there was a rise of several degrees.

As usual, Corman's confidence was making Larsen squirm. It didn't seem possible that the old man could have hoaxed him again, in spite of all the precautions, but Larsen was obviously unhappy.

Finally the tenth reading was given and recorded, and Larsen called his helpers in. When the two lists were compared, they stood as follows:

Number	Corman's Estimate	Thermometer
1.	82	80.6
2.	82	80.9
3.	75	75.4
4.	75	74.8
5.	74	74.2
6.	71	71.5
7.	76	77.3
8.	71	72.0
9.	71	71.7
10.	70	70.6

I think Lambert was more crestfallen than Larsen; the latter half expected it, I felt, and no longer hoped to win against the old man.

Lambert loudly derided the ESP explanation, and tried to make Corman give the true one, but all he got was a gentle comment: "There are more things in heaven and earth, Horatio—pardon me; I mean Ken—but you know the quote. What I can't understand is why Larsen is so opposed to the ESP theory; usually, he's always plumping for it!"

Larsen gritted his teeth, but said nothing.

For the first time, I had no inkling of the solution, myself, but meant to find out. And I did, by cornering the old man a few days later, and blocking his way to the water cooler.

"I'm thirsty as hell," Corman said, "so you've got me over a barrel. Now if I were twenty years younger, my lad, I'd flip you over that desk! Not that I'd hoped to keep the secret much longer. There must be *somebody* around here who knows something besides physical science."

"Meaning?" I prompted him.

"Meaning that biology can be useful, too. I had help on the outside—a thousand to one against Larsen's two."

I gaped at him.

"It's not very well known," he went on, "at least among mathematicians, astronomers, and physicists, but there are simple formulas connecting air temperature with the chirping frequency of certain species of crickets. For one kind here, it's merely this: Count the number of chirps in fifteen seconds, and add forty. The sum is the temperature in degrees Fahrenheit. You'll find it in Lutz, and also Pierce's book, 'The Songs of Insects.' "

"As simple as that," I said. Then, puzzled: "But you couldn't see the clock."

"I'm surprised at you," he told me reproachfully. "Forgetting Galileo and his pendulum so easily. A man's pulse, once he's checked it out, is an ideal timer. My own, for example, beats at a steady rate of seventy per minute—at least, in the early evening. In other words seven beats every six seconds."

I reflected for a moment.

"For eighty degrees, then, you must have counted forty chirps in fifteen seconds—isn't that hard to do?"

"Not with practice. Anybody can count aloud faster than that."

"So that's why you clasped your hands—you were taking your own pulse!"

"Naturally."

"What if Larsen had plugged your ears?"

"It's not easy to keep out those shrill chirps; you noted, subconsciously, I'm sure, how they came right through the walls, even. Now, if he'd tied my hands behind me; or if the temperature had dropped below seventy ..."

"Below forty, the formula must fail; you'd have to subtract, instead of add. But why seventy?"

He grinned.

"Biology again. Most crickets won't sing when the temperature goes below seventy. Larsen would have had me—ah—cold!"

Degree Candidate

"The candidate may enter."

Jav tensed. Now that the time had come, he felt uneasy. Little was known of these special qualification councils. Successful candidates were sworn to secrecy. There might even be an investigator's report, and Jav's conscience was not clear, no matter how much he might rationalize the situation.

But this was no time to show any doubt; the examiners were waiting. Jav took comfort from the fact that his record as a brilliant, if somewhat erratic, student must be well known to the council. After all, it was on the basis of past performance that he had been given a free hand with a major project. Not many students as young as he were ever assigned a whole experimental unit for their research.

He permitted energy to flow in vibrant quanta through certain networks of his complex, multidimensional structure, and found himself in the audience chamber.

The examiners hovered there, thoughts perfectly shielded, some maintaining invisibility of the highest order, others content to be grossly tangible on a wide spectrum.

"The Candidate Jav, aspirant for a Class Three Degree." A junior examiner projected the thought, gemlike in its hard clarity.

A more authoritative pattern was formed: "The candidate will report on his project." The Chief Examiner had taken charge.

Jav deflected energy packets into vortices charged with his summary. Smoothly the specialized radiators released precise wavelengths holding millions of information units. It was skillfully done, a vast amount of material expertly integrated, but the officials appeared unimpressed. Were they actually unfriendly, or merely blasé?

Jav's uneasy conscience gave him no rest. There were iron laws binding experimenters; if you let them overawe you, destroying your initiative, the project couldn't amount to much. Yet he had to satisfy their highly exacting demands within the framework of rigid ethical considerations. If he failed to do so, there would be no degree, and he might suffer the deep humiliation of a new, less difficult assignment. The old one would be turned over to a better student, or possibly abandoned altogether.

He stopped his sub-thoughts momentarily to check on the data vortices. They were functioning perfectly. He sensed their fleeting aside: "—dependent upon the element oxygen. No such form of life has been studied before—" He tuned out. Next would come the claim that a Class Eleven Intelligence had been evolved by his methods. That was a critical point. Actually it was nearer to Class Thirteen, but he felt sure of getting away with the exaggeration. A check would require much time. As a matter of fact, if he had tended more strictly to business, even a Class Nine might have been reached. The creatures, when properly handled, were remarkably susceptible to improvement. Was it the oxygen? One more question he should have cleared up instead of—oh, well, the Council wasn't likely to check up. Too many candidates up for their degrees. He'd get back to real work, and with any luck, could soon have the facts in perfect accord with his official report.

Cautiously, with the utmost delicacy, Jav extended his sensory pattern until it brushed the Chief Examiner's aura, lightly as a shadow flickers over stone. His tautness eased. The Chief was not hostile. Unless, Jav reflected, he was deliberately modifying the shield. And surely no mere aspirant was important enough for that. If the Chief Examiner *were* pleased, that coveted degree was practically his. The vortices were concluding: "—very effective environment … swift evolution … Eleventh Class in a single time-unit—" A few final thought waves, neatly modulated, rippled free. The end of his report.

There was a moment's absence of all projection, then the Chief Examiner commanded: "Let the Investigator begin."

Jav shrank within himself, dimensionality blurred. So there *was* an investigator. It had been rumored that only a minute percentage of the experiments were ever checked—those of weaker students, normally. How carefully had this official probed? Perhaps he'd made only a routine, superficial survey. Maybe—

The first question flew lancelike into his being. "Candidate Jav, what is Rule Three of the Code?"

Was that merely a test of his knowledge, or direct accusation? How much did they really know? He remained calm, quoting glibly, without tapping any vortices for data stored formally: "Every manifestation of life, however simple, is entitled to freedom from all pain except that irreducible residue attendant on the metabolic processes themselves."

The swift counter shattered any illusions about the motive behind that first question.

"Do you deny inflicting upon the organisms of your project pain and suffering of the sort specifically barred by Rule Three?"

Jav's thought patterns quivered with erratic current surges. The answer came. "No, but such torment was necessary in order to determine the full potentialities of the creatures under investigation." He was instantly aware of the pulse of disapproval that flashed through the Council. Was everything lost? A direct lie would have been fatal. Better to try a justification. Maybe that's all they wanted, a bold defense—intellectual courage.

"Surely the candidate knows that no further data about life, even if so attainable, excuses such barbaric maltreatment of lower animals. And that more than enough facts were accumulated before adoption of the Code to prove that pain is never anything but a deterrent to the development of high lifeforms. Why, then, did you revert to a class of experiments long since forbidden as cruel and fruitless?"

"I was aware of the earlier researches, but not convinced they had exhausted so valuable a field." He groped for further arguments. "If I have erred," he declared boldly, "it was only through desire for knowledge, and not because I lacked compassion for my primitive organisms."

"You pretend, then, that parasitic diseases, famine, and—ultimate horror—war, were allowed to rage among these miserable creatures only to improve our understanding of life?"

"I do." There was no hope now except to brazen it out. If he'd dreamed they were going to check so thoroughly …

"If that was so," the Investigator went on relentlessly, "what was the purpose—" here the thought was charged with searing scorn—"of appearing in various physical guises on the very mud-daub of the experimental area? Why, Candidate Jav, did you degrade yourself to play Personal God to these pitiful animals? Why did you match one group against the other, accepting, even soliciting their primitive, superstitious 'worship'? Was it for knowledge, or because you enjoyed the role? Speak!"

Jav remained miserably thoughtless, currents clashing aimlessly about the vortices.

The Investigator continued. "What of the Crusades? The Thirty Years' War? The Black Death? Dachau? The ghosts, witches, vampires—odd creations of your leisure moments. All for knowledge, no doubt!"

It was all over; Jav didn't reply. Why *had* he used those animals for dalliance, amusement? Was it because even in their brutishness, they had just enough godliness to excite his resentment? No, not that, surely. It was their reactions, their absurd illogic that had tempted him. Their weird behavior was so fascinating, he had simply lost sight of his original goals. They reminded him of a mathematics theorem which gives back something different, unexpected—more than you put into it, so to speak. They spoke all together in acceptance of a particular belief; but when you raided their pitiful minds, you found delightful contradictions. Like the time he'd been all those silly, too human Greek Gods. The idiots would promise Zeus an ox, and gleefully hoodwink him with some burned entrails, while eating the good meat themselves. Accept a being as all powerful, then stupidly believe you could outwit him in such a childish way.

And, after all, most of the cruelty was theirs, not his. He had merely stirred up certain innate tendencies. But then he had made them as they were, or, at least, failed to guide their evolution properly. Well, it was too late now. He should have followed the Code. Ironically enough, now that he could never return, he felt a sudden perverse affection for the filthy, quarrelsome, treacherous, brutal, and stupid organisms he had created so casually. He could even recall instances of courage and faith that were touching. Take Daniel, for example. Those lions couldn't scare him. Or that young girl—a child—who had allowed herself to be tortured to death rather than confess falsely that she was a witch. Older, stronger men and women had submitted ... Then there was Newton, Shakespeare, Beethoven. Pity, the way things were turning out.

The Investigator attacked again. "Were you not also guilty, in a fit of irrational annoyance, of destroying the whole experiment by means of a flood? Why wasn't that reported officially, as the Code prescribes?"

Jav dropped all defense in a plea for mercy. If they would only let him, he would instantly ameliorate the creatures' lot. He would soften their harsh environment, prevent nuclear wars, teach them love and forbearance, raise their brutish souls to the stars. His wave pattern, no longer well modulated, vibrated wildly. He would—

The Chief Examiner broke in coldly. "It is too late. The candidate is failed. In addition he is barred forever from further work towards the degree. His plea for rehabilitation of these unfortunate primitives is herewith denied, since such a program would inevitably entail excessive suffering after so much damage. Surely these creatures deserve our crowning mercy, late though it is." He sent out a peremptory call: "Ga'r'el!"

"I await your commands, Chief Examiner."

"Go immediately to the Galaxy of Experiment. Project 45-R-16 is on Planet III of Solar Model 4,788,653,229. See that every trace of life is destroyed instantly, without pain. Wipe the surface clean. This Council is adjourned."

The Auto Hawks

They came from the Santa Ana Hills. You couldn't have found a better man to explain the whole thing. I was Professor of Zoology at Cal Tech then. Emeritus, now. Light up, and I'll give you the real facts. The so-called histories are wrong on many details.

One thing is certain; the hawks appeared right here in California first. May, 1965—that's almost the exact date of the start. They branched out fast enough, but were most successful in the West, for reasons you'll see. It's a bit ironical, too, that California, which claims to have the largest this, and most gigantic that, isn't too proud of its most authentic giants.

The first attack occurred in May of 1965, as I've said. I have the account in my notebook. All science begins with somebody's jottings, incidentally. Because of my complete, detailed records, I was able to pick out the clues that led to a solution.

The joke is, nobody believed the original report. Reminds me of the Wright Brothers' experience, when it took months for the few witnesses, reputable as they were, to make people in other parts of the country accept the fact that something tremendous happened at Kitty Hawk.

About ten persons saw this auto hawk in action. They were in the three cars just behind the victim, on the El Toro Road. The only reason the "News" printed their account, I suspect, is that the Liars' Club was meeting then in Los Angeles, and it seemed to fit in. But anyhow these people all agreed that this monster hawk, the size of a bomber, came swooping down and snatched that new Chrysler smack off the road. Frankly, in their place, I wouldn't have had the nerve to tell anybody, least of all a reporter. You could get put away for sticking to a story like that.

But actually they were safe in talking, since verification came fast. Before long, many people had seen the automobile hawks at work, and the doubters got squelched. When your own Aunt Lil or nephew Ricky was involved, that settled it. Back East, at first, they were more skeptical; there was the usual talk about L.A. as an open-air booby-hatch.

The hawks multiplied fast—optimal conditions, biologists call it. You've seen a few photos and mounted specimens, but not many people remember how they flew. They were a lot like ordinary hawks, except for size. They'd hover, rocking in the updraft, and you'd see the sun flash red on the flanges of their tails as they banked, graceful and smooth. Then a lightning, precise stoop, just like a sparrow hawk taking a mouse. To an ornithologist, especially an underpaid professor who was still driving a 1959 heap, there were worse sights than a big, handsome hawk whistling down to scoop a $6,000 convertible off the highway!

Lord! The questions the whole situation raised. First, what in blazes did a hawk want with an auto? And where did they acquire such a taste all of a sudden? It couldn't be instinct, you see.

Well, as for the taste, we learned later that the birds picked it up around some used car graveyards in the area of Los Angeles and its environs. A few young ones brought up on such—ah—Detroit carrion, shall we say?—that was the genesis.

For a while nobody took it too seriously. With hundreds of people killed daily in crashes, the few cars grabbed by auto hawks didn't seem to matter much. After all, it was obvious that the big birds weren't after people as such. A few died through falling from their cars when the hawks hoisted them; but before long California drivers learned that when you heard a mighty swoosh through the air, it was best to pull over and pile out—but fast. You couldn't teach the breed to observe speed laws, or lay off the popskull before driving, but this they learned in a hurry. Even the wild kids.

I think the first real squawks of anguish came from the used car dealers. It seems that young hawks, many of them raised on junked cars and not too sure of their powers, preferred to raid the lots. It was the easiest target—no timing required. A young bird could easily miss its first dive at a fast-moving car on the road. And such a blunder could hurt, since like as not the car behind would bat him in the tail feathers. Quite a few were crippled that way.

Now, by this time, with the menace snowballing, we—the biologists—were learning some amazing things about these unique birds. As I said, they were breeding in considerable numbers here in the Santa Ana Hills. I ask you, what part of the country offered more to an auto hawk than Southern California? Talk about ideal conditions! As you'll see, those brushy hills were vital; in less sheltered places, with a different climate—political and geographical—man would soon have the upper hand. Here, the birds had it.

Gradually, ornithologists and ranchers began to accumulate data. There was no question about the motive any more: the hawks were actually *eating* automobiles. Or I should say parts of them. There was one big fellow with a barred tail, for example, that wouldn't touch anything but hoods. He'd snatch a car off the highway, carry it up about half a mile, and then drop it on the rocks by Seal Point. Every half hour, almost, you'd hear the crash. Like a seagull with clams. Then he'd hustle down and pick over the pieces, especially bits of the hood. Others went for dashboards, panels, or what have you. But never any of the metal parts—that was so significant we should have caught it earlier. A few birds preferred tires, even though they meant hard work. The hawks had remarkably powerful bills, but even so, ripping off the casing—all wire and tough synthetic rubber good for five million miles—to get at the inside, was a tiresome, lengthy chore.

On the whole, there was bound to be a lot of waste, too. No hawk ever ate more than, say, fifteen per cent of each car. And they wouldn't bother with each other's leavings either. Unfortunately, the other eighty-five per cent wasn't worth salvaging after hitting the rocks from two thousand feet up. Yes, the birds were fussy, and why not? The roads were literally choked with cars, so they could take their pick. Besides, like any healthy predator, they enjoyed attacking moving objects.

Nowadays, years after, people ask why more wasn't done. Well, to begin with, it would have been reasonable, on the surface, to get some planes from the armed forces and blow hell out of the nests, either with bombs or rockets. If that could have been done early enough, the whole business might have been prevented.

But it wasn't quite that simple—politics, among other things, were involved. You know what ranchers in California suffer from fires. These long, dry summers have always been murder. Can you imagine them letting a bunch of fly-boys start blazes on every brushy hill in the Santa Ana range? Places it was almost impossible to reach with fire-fighting equipment? The farmers and ranchers didn't care a damn about the motorists—mostly tourists, anyhow—and they raised such hell in Sacramento that the governor called off the planes.

Oh, a few of the hawks were shot down, in the beginning, by naval airmen out on patrols; they were a pushover for jet fighters and rockets; but the birds began taking it out on transports and private planes. Don't ask me if they figured it out logically; I don't know. Maybe they got a hate on against planes, but found that only certain kinds could be tackled with any chance of success. I do know this: gradually there was a kind of truce. If the jets didn't kill any hawks for a few days, the commercial planes weren't bothered. The missile bases got in some good target practice, but the government howled. The birds weren't fast enough to double for enemy rockets, and cost $200,000 each. It just didn't make sense, economically. So all this wasn't helping the guy who drove all the way from Ham Hocks, Indiana, to see Liz Taylor's house.

Not that Californians gave up the fight. All sorts of schemes were tried. Used car dealers had the simplest problem. It's easy to protect a lot, where all the cars are concentrated in a small area, and motionless. Before long all the "Saintly Sams" and "Noble Nudelmans" in California had war surplus .50 caliber machine guns strategically spotted in all their lots, and the hawks learned to stay away.

But the best most motorists could manage was a 12-gauge shotgun, and it took a sharpshooter with a cool head to get a hawk that came hurtling down from nowhere at 150 miles an hour. A brain shot was necessary, otherwise Mr. Hawk just combed the pellets out of his feathers and kept coming. And if you didn't stop the bird, there was no time to scramble out of the car, which could mean your finish. There were human remains as well as those of cars on the rocks. So individuals didn't fight back to any extent; it just didn't pay.

Then people tried the convoy system. A few armored cars would herd fifty or sixty autos along Highway 101. But although it worked perfectly, after a few hawks had been blasted, nobody liked the system except the Nervous Nellies. They just didn't care to follow a timetable, all rolling along at fifty. Junior couldn't always wait to relieve himself; Martha was starving, and the group wasn't due to stop for an hour. Besides, not all of them wanted to stay on 101.

So there were enough cars on the smaller roads at all times to feed a million hawks.

The birds got even fussier and more arrogant. There was one undersized devil—runt of the nest, probably—that went for the little cars. I used to watch him with my binoculars from the biology office at the college. He had a nest right there—yes, under that reddish boulder just below the crest. He ate nothing but Isettas, so help me—what part I never knew. One day I saw him carry out a real coup—an Isetta in each foot, something that couldn't happen with big cars. One of the drivers fired a whole pistol-full at him, but the gun was only a .22 from the sound of it, and the poor fool might just as well have tried spitballs.

There were other, obvious expedients. A few cars were booby-trapped with explosives, and blasted some hawks. But that was picayune stuff. People tied bags of arsenic in strategic places on their cars, too. They may have killed a handful of birds. But most families have children, and if you have any poison within a mile of a child, he'll manage to eat it. The same child who won't eat his nice healthy dinner for anything! So most people didn't mess with poison, either.

It got to the point where the only safe vehicles were busses—their business was phenomenal that year—and small stuff: bicycles, scooters—as well as the big trucks, although once in a while an ambitious red-tail might tip over an empty.

As I've said, hunting them with planes wasn't practicable. You can't send a Mach 2 jet cavorting around between rocky peaks. If the hawk had sense enough to hug the passes, which most of them learned to do soon, no plane could get at him; and even with a clear shot, the pilot didn't dare fire because of all the dry brush waiting to go up in smoke. True, the rainy season was coming, but by that time we had the answer anyway. In the East, of course, jets did a good job of clean up.

One bright spot was the fact that the hawks didn't fly at night. If there'd been any auto owls, that would have been rough. As it was, you could drive safely after dark.

Well, the ending is better known than the beginning, so I won't drag it out. My notes gave me the first clue, which was the absolute immunity of cars built before 1962. I had to find out why this was so. What changes, if any, had occurred in that year? At that point, the clue became a mile-high fingerpost.

You may not remember, a young fellow like you, how we suffered from crop surpluses, but they were a terrible problem. There were hundreds of huge warehouses bulging with tons of wheat and corn; the maintenance of such places was in itself a heavy financial burden.

Then, in 1961, a chemist at the University of Chicago discovered how to make a cheap, attractive plastic from these surplus grains. It was ideal for auto construction. There had been plastic-bodied sport cars before, but always in the luxury class. Now a body molded of Flexine was cast for almost nothing compared to other materials. The government was delighted to sell the wheat and corn without ruining farm prices, and our crop surplus problem disappeared.

Well, that was the first clue. Naturally, a plastic made of grain could be highly nutritious, but not enough, it would seem, to make giants out of ordinary birds.

I got a grant, and went deeper into the problem with the Chemistry Department. We analyzed hundreds of samples of Flexine before realizing what we were looking for.

Nowadays everybody knows about gibberellin, the growth element discovered in the 1950s. Even in 1960 it was being used to produce larger wheat and corn plants—in spite of the surplus. Well, gibberellin was present in Flexine, but certainly, we thought, in too small quantities to have such an effect on the hawks. The percent of the stuff was well under two-tenths, but other material in the Flexine acted as a booster.

The whole picture was now clear. Hungry young hawks, during a year of high rabbit mortality, nibbled plastic in auto graveyards. The gibberellin and booster made them into giants, and they turned to snatching cars off the road.

The solution was easy. Gibberellin was processed out of the plastic, and the next generation of hawks was normal in size. They could eat all of the stuff they could get, now, but it wouldn't make them grow any more than rabbit or mouse meat.

And that's the whole story, young fellow. The scourge lasted only eleven months, but this country will never forget the Year of the Hawks.

Revenge

If the Syndicate is half as powerful as some people have claimed, they'll murder me any day now. I object on principle to being killed by evil men for a good deed, so maybe lynching by stupid ones is preferable. I mean you, and you—the suetheads who profited by my work, but refused your help.

You've been yammering about narcotics for years—how drug addiction was spreading, reaching down even to your unmannerly, spoiled brats, who despise their parents and our venal society to the same degree. The stuff comes in by the ton across the Mexican border; they grow it for our benefit in Red China; and a few "friendly" Asian countries don't mind exporting some now and then, either. In spite of heroic work by our small group of poorly financed narcotics agents, the flow of drugs cannot be halted.

Oh, you and your elected representatives made a lot of panicky moves to combat this threat. The Department of Health, Education, and Welfare was given a new Bureau, set up like the F.B.I., and headed by Myron P. Bishop, a man trained by that distinguished expert on narcotics, Anslinger, himself.

But as to sensible solutions, such as legalizing the sale of heroin to break the worldwide criminal control on the distribution of drugs— that your vapid Puritan morality wouldn't permit. Millions of dollars for enforcement, and to punish the sick, but not one cent for prevention, and almost nothing to find out why people become addicts in the first place, and how to cure them.

It wasn't entirely your fault. You listened to the experts, usually career policemen who expect to cure any social evil with clubs and prisons. I am reminded of the simpleton found measuring two horses with a tape in order to be able to distinguish the black one from the white. Until I came along, nobody had ever reached the core of the matter. You don't kill a flourishing plant—in this case a Upas Tree—by lopping off a handful of leaves. You strike at the roots. That's what I meant to do—and did—for your benefit. Oh, I admit there were a few dollars in it for me, but so what? The ox that treads the wheat is not muzzled. When a man saves a manufacturer $50,000 a year by some improved process, or even by using three bolts someplace instead of four, they gladly pay him three per cent of the annual savings, or something like that, as a reward. Most big outfits have such a policy, and it's a good one. Well, if I cut millions off the government budget, is a lousy $100,000 too much to ask? I just wanted to go on with my researches without battling a horde of bill collectors every month. Fat chance—I didn't get a measly dime. You, your elected and appointed officials, and your kept press just gave me the all-time horselaugh. Well, he who laughs last—you'll remember the old saw; I'll see to that.

I'm writing this so you'll know how they treated me. You mustn't think I'm a crank, mad at the world for no reason. My case is better than Dreyfus' and Sacco-Vanzetti's combined. Here I was prepared to remove the drug scourge forever, and at a piddling cost. Did I get courteous handling, or at least a fair hearing? Not bloody likely! I was an idiot to expect anything from the world's most inflated bureaucracy—Dickens' Circumlocution Office brought up to date.

Let me start at the beginning; then you'll see who's right. I'm a biochemist by profession. A damned good one, but too individualistic to please the big research centers. They like docile teams—scientific Percherons to pull the big red wagon. So I taught at one jerkwater college after another. Sooner or later my superiors, all dodderers who stopped thinking with sighs of relief once they had their PhD union cards, objected to my attitude. If I published, they were jealous; it made the other faculty members look bad. If I failed to produce, then why was I wasting lab facilities and neglecting my classes? The students wanted their term papers back within five days; the other teachers could manage it, why not me? The difference between what my colleagues expected from their pupils and what I did was the difference between the lightning bug and the lightning. Those students! They didn't want biochemistry; they want a letter on a card; a "C" would do. Damn few of them got it from me, I'm happy to say, and those that did, knew more about the subject than most PhD's.

Now, I take as my creed the fruitful dictum: Think in other categories. A famous researcher once invented—or discovered—this maxim in a dream. It is the secret of many great advances in science. Get off the main line. Stop fooling with the leaves of the tree, and turn to the roots. Invert the problem, if necessary.

I was thinking about the narcotics scandal. A teacher at my college had a lovely sixteen-year-old daughter, carefully reared, who was badly hooked. I saw that poor man's hair whiten in a few months. How would you feel, knowing that your daughter had been so degraded by a drug as to sell herself to anybody with enough money to buy her a fix? An innocent, playful sniff at a party, and some punk, probably an addict himself, had trapped her in order to finance his own habit. They talk about cures, but people on the inside know that permanent escape from the trap is as rare as portraits of Trotsky in Russia. Or integrity among politicians in this country.

Well, I put my brains to work on the problem. It seemed obvious that, as in the case of Prohibition, you couldn't possibly lick the drug traffic by cutting the lines of supply. Not in a country as big as ours, with the Mexican border and Red China on the side of the enemy. Not when a package the size of a watch could be worth a fortune.

Think in other categories, I reminded myself. How can a biochemist, rather than a policeman, stop the Syndicate? Then it came to me, simple and obvious. Hit the source, the weak link, the roots of the poison tree. In short, *Papaver somniferum*, the opium poppy itself.

Basic, isn't it? Destroy the plant, and you cut the heart out of the drug traffic. No cops; no hopeless warfare against cunning smugglers; no battle with big-money corruption of officials. And remember: no chemist alive can synthesize opium or its derivatives. Sure, there are a few other bad narcotic drugs from different plants, like marijuana, but they play a relatively small part, and can be controlled. Besides, it was my intention to destroy their sources as well, when the time came. But first the biggest culprit.

I got to work, re-examining all the recent work on tobacco virus and similar plant killers. New studies on the key protein chains of the genes were the foundation stones of my plan. The disease had to be highly specific and deadly. I couldn't risk even the remotest possibility of harming food plants in a hungry world.

But, as I've said, with no false modesty, I'm no slouch in my field of biochemistry. I took a harmless poppy rust from our California flowers here, and treated its genes with certain chemicals. It was a matter of six months, and well over eighty tries, but finally I came up with a virus that killed the opium poppy like smallpox wiped out the Sioux. No; more than that. Some Indians were, or became, immune to the disease, just as insects build up resistance to the most potent poisons. But with my virus that's simply not possible. I won't get technical here, but to become immune to this stuff would be like a man's developing anti-bodies against his own tissues. It couldn't happen without killing the organism faster than the virus does. Once this epidemic began, not a poppy would survive.

So far everything was fine, except that, as usual, I lost my job. I got fifty term papers behind. It didn't bother me, because there wasn't a student in my three classes who knew any more biochemistry than a baboon. In the first paper I'd found this gem: "It is well known that a mammal reproduces by suckling its young." Faced with more of the same, it was a pleasure to be fired.

Now, in any really civilized society, they'd have my statue on top of the Capitol building, and with neon lights to boot. But in our bureaucratic wilderness of Washington, with a thousand government-hired cretins running interference for each big, appointed super-cretin, my troubles had just begun.

I took some sample poppies to the H.E.W. offices. They were in vacuum sealed plastic envelopes, because I knew that once my virus spores got loose in the atmosphere, they'd spread all over the world like radioactive dust, or faster. I hoped to see the Commissioner of Narcotics, Myron P. Bishop, but His Magnificence was harder to reach than the whole College of Cardinals. It was impossible to put my point across. Plants, was it? That way to the Department of Agriculture. Oh, poppies. Pamphlets on wildflowers could be had from Documents.

I wrote countless letters, pulled what few wires were within my reach, and haunted Washington like the ghost of Calhoun. And finally I got ten minutes with El Pomposo himself.

As I've said, dumb students are nothing new to me. But even the worst of them couldn't have been any more obtuse than Bishop. I had the dead plants, all brown and withered. There were simple charts showing exactly, in terms of time, how the virus worked, killing the poppy within forty-eight hours, and even destroying the viability of any seeds that might be ripening.

Did this jughead appointed by the President to fight the terrible drug problem comprehend the miracle being offered to him? The simple solution that would make him the greatest—in fact, the only—success in his post that this country had ever known? Not he. I had to spell it out in nursery school terms.

But I've penetrated many a numbskull in class by dint of persistent drilling, and finally got through to the cold oatmeal under his parietal bones.

Did that clear the air? If you think so, guess again. He threw up his hands in horror. Turn a plant disease loose on the world deliberately! It was a violation of the conventions against germ warfare. It was barred by international law. It was unthinkable that the United States would indulge in such irresponsible behavior.

All right, I said. Take it to the U.N. Let them distribute the poppy killer. He brightened a little at that, since every bureaucrat loves above all to pass the buck. A clear-cut decision is fatal to the species. Then he gave me a note to our delegate, Wilbur Cavanaugh, Jr.

This character was a bit sharper. He heard me out, looked at my deceased poppies, and arranged a conference with a bigwig from the State Department. Then things got really messy. When I pointed out that in a few weeks every damned opium plant in Asia would be deader than the Ming Dynasty, this little creep from Foggy Bottom almost had kittens on the spot. It seems that just now our relations with Red China are highly delicate. If we turned the virus loose on them, even if it did kill only poppies (and he had his doubts about that. What if—shudder—it attacked rice?) the Reds would scream murder.

They'd yell germ warfare, and have us cold. They could ship us opium by the long ton—that didn't affect the delicate condition, though.

It seemed to me, however, that there was something ambiguous and wistful in the State man's attitude, and I thought I understood. When a country sends a spy to do some dirty job, they disown him officially if he is caught. Except for that U-2 fiasco some years ago, when the U.S. broke all the unwritten rules and made jackasses of us before the world. Now, obviously, if I killed all the poppies in the world, that would be a *fait accompli*. Washington could deny knowing anything about the cause of death, especially since it would work indiscriminately even in friendly parts of Asia. Just as long as I got my hundred thousand, I didn't mind skipping the official credit. In fact, it would keep the Syndicate off my back.

"Suppose," I said, "on my own responsibility, I release the spores and ruin the opium trade for good. Will you see that I get paid?"

He was horrified. In the first place, nothing whatever could be done until the virus had been checked out by government scientists. If I would give him the virus, and my notes, he'd start the ball rolling. I know that Washington ball; it's all angles, and doesn't roll worth a damn. I went cold at the thought. Before you can get an okay on anything big from a bureau there, your long, grey beard will be sweeping the floor.

For a moment I was tempted to take my plans to England, but then remembered that by sane legislation legalizing the sale of drugs under controlled conditions, they had already licked the problem, and wouldn't be in the market. For two cents, I thought, I'd make China pay me the money to keep the virus buried. For that matter, the Syndicate would gladly kick in with a million. But I'm an American first, and couldn't play it that way, especially remembering Professor A's daughter.

I thought the thing through, and decided that if I turned the disease loose, so that every good poppy is a dead one, any decent government will quietly pay me off. They only need to know that no other plants are affected.

And that's the way I played it. The next day I sprayed a few grams of concentrated virus into the humid air of Washington, and went home. If you read the papers, you know the rest of that particular story. In eight months not even Sherlock Holmes could have found a live opium poppy on the face of the Earth. Once current stocks are gone, there'll be no more narcotics deriving from that particular plant. The government sensibly outbid all the addicts and operators in order to save what is left for medical use. It should last for fifty years. All according to my plan—fine!

But when I tried to collect, they didn't know me from the late Lucky Luciano. There was no proof whatever, they said, that my virus did the job. After all, their scientists had not been allowed to check my work. I could have faked the whole thing, attempting to take credit for a mutant disease which began naturally, especially since dozens of bacteriologists were now isolating the virus.

When I pressed harder, they dragged out an F.B.I. file showing I was a crank and maverick, unable to hold a job, and guilty of signing a peace petition in 1949. If Bishop or Cavanaugh tried to help, I don't know about it. I suppose I'm lucky that the Syndicate has been equally skeptical. Otherwise, being out many millions, they would have liquidated me by now.

But basically it's your fault—you, the people. I took my case to you, as a court of last resort. A few papers gave me a fair enough shake to present the evidence, but you paid no attention. I tried to get your signatures to a petition to purge the H.E.W. Department, or to start a Congressional investigation. You just laughed at me. You enjoyed that headline: "Crackpot Chemist Claims He Killed All Those Poppies. Was it Self Defense?"

Well, my jovial friends, I'm going to teach you a lesson. I could easily wipe out half of you by killing some selected food plants, but I'm not a mass murderer, and would rather make a more subtle job of it. I've two more viruses just about perfected; after the first, it's easier. When I turn them loose, you'll have a real grievance against me. This time, you're getting notice in advance, so nobody can talk about "natural" disease. Besides, the appended lab notes will easily convince a few key men in biochemistry; and they'll confirm me.

Now let me point out the two plants you'll miss badly.

One is yeast. Yes, yeast. When you read this, the one-celled organisms responsible for wine, beer, and alcohol generally, will be dying as a race. In a few months, good liquor will be scarcer than an electric blanket in hell. Sure, grain alcohol can be synthesized, but bouquet isn't that simple, and you'll pay dearly for it—how you'll pay! And decent lab-made whiskey won't be on the shelves tomorrow, either.

The other plant you'll miss even more. I mean tobacco. No more cigarettes; no more fat cigars—and hallelujah!—no more tobacco commercials on TV. Did you know, tobacco cannot be synthesized at all, at any price? Get it, you two-pack-a-day fiends?

Off His Rocker

I want to clear up this confusion right now—there isn't much time left. For the city, I mean. You can feel it even out here, and we're—how far?—at least three miles away. See that vase quiver? Before long it'll be rocking eight, ten degrees. That's not a temblor, no matter what they say. If the *Record* building holds together much longer, don't be surprised to lose this place, too.

Hell! You still don't believe a word. You think I'm crazy. Well, I'm not. I didn't file forty-nine top patents because I'm feebleminded. Unless you show some sense in a hurry, and use your influence to do something soon, more houses are going to collapse. They go first—no steel frames. Look, all you have to do is send somebody to my office—ten twelve—there's a little switch on the wall behind the desk. Just have him press the black button, and everything will be over. He'll need to be a guy with guts and good coordination, because by now that floor must be swaying thirty or more degrees from the vertical. Don't run out on me now—you're the only one who can save the center of town. Don't look at me that way; I'm no crazier than you are. Maybe if I start from the beginning …

One month ago today, that's when it started. The *Los Angeles Record* sent that wise guy reporter to cover the gadgets in my "miracle" house. That's what the neighbors call it.

He asked me a lot of questions, and I gave him straight answers. I don't believe in false modesty. What I'm doing will eventually make Einstein seem a baby by comparison. I'm getting really close to the secrets of gravitation and electromagnetism.

But all this young fool could do was make fun of my gadgets. You may have seen the article he wrote; it made me look like a damned idiot. I wrote a sharp letter. They chopped it up to give the worst impression. From then on, they never let up on me.

I decided to contact the editor; he's Harvey Brace Lemon. There was no reply to my note. I tried to see him in person; they gave me the runaround. A reporter obviously hoped to get me mad so he could fake up another unfair story.

I thought of suing, but knew that would be a waste of time. Nobody wins against a big paper. They can tie up the case for years with their top lawyers, so that it costs you thousands of dollars to get a hearing. Then, even if they lose, you're likely to end up with a lousy dollar and a hypocritical apology. Besides, people like that are insured against libel suits. I didn't want insurance company money—I was out for their mangy hides.

Then I got the idea of dealing with the publisher. Maybe he wasn't aware of their scummy tactics. He has the power to take steps. I wired him at Carmel, where he has a mansion or two. He never bothered to answer, even when I tried a couple more times.

I was beginning to get mad. It was clear that the whole staff was to blame. Probably the publisher himself set the tone.

As a last resort, I stated my case to the other papers in town. Fat lot of good that did. They wouldn't print a word. One paper will never oppose another on behalf of a third party, no matter how hotly they may feud among themselves.

Well, now I was really mad. Constant misrepresentation and arrogance—that's what it is—plain, nasty arrogance; the public be damned. Too big for their breeches, those executives of the *Record*.

Now I don't get angry very easily; I'm a tolerant guy. In scientific work, you've got to be open-minded; to get along with all kinds. I cooperate with any type of people: radicals, reactionaries, cranks, neurotics, sour old maids, and wild-eyed playboys. We're all human, and as Mark Twain cracked, that's so bad in itself that nothing worse can be cited against us.

But when I really get my Irish up—not that I'm Irish; that's just an expression—things happen fast. That damn newspaper infuriated me with its unfairness, and I figured I'd teach them a lesson about public relations they wouldn't forget in a hurry.

But here am I, a lousy physicist—really, I'm a good one; a genius; I mean, though, what's an individual against a bunch of power-drunk pirates like that? Society puts all its weight on their side. What could one man accomplish with a whole oligarchy of money and prestige? The *Record*, biggest paper on the West Coast. Printing plant in a new fifty-story building that cost millions. What would happen, by the way, if you or I wanted to build a skyscraper here in Los Angeles? Zoning laws didn't permit it; too many earthquakes in this area. But the *Record* changes that ordinance in a hurry. A few quiet words to the City Fathers are all it takes. Of course, they did erect a good, solid steel structure, so that the danger was negligible.

Well, that's when I got an idea. If I could wreck their nice new building, it would knock some of the arrogance out of them fast, and get in a good blow for other people they'd lied about.

I began to consider the problem seriously. A tough proposition, you'll agree. I doubt if anybody else in the world could have solved it. Real genius is called for. I could rent an office in their building easily enough, but then what? Start a fire? I thought of that; but the automatic sprinklers would kill it in no time; and even if I jimmied up the ones around my floor, the flames wouldn't do much damage. Besides, they have insurance. They might be inconvenienced, but the underwriters would take the real loss, and I had nothing against them.

Explosives? It would take a whole freight train to carry enough to wreck a modern steel structure like that. And, anyway, I'm not callous; you mustn't think that. Why do you suppose I'm trying to stop the mess now? An explosion would have hurt innocent people and their property—even Billy Button fans.

I thought of blowing up just the presses, but the floor was crowded with people day and night. And insurance was still involved. You can't even put the fool paper out of business for a few weeks; they'd probably get to use the *Mirror's* presses temporarily. Publishers help each other that way, even though they're red-hot rivals. So I seemed to be up against a dead end.

But in my work, that's nothing new. When Oldenburger and I tried to design a new missile governor to operate with a point zero zero three per cent variation at 1,500 degrees Fahrenheit, we backed out of at least six blind alleys, and still found a solution. There's always a way past, around, or under.

But fire wouldn't do, nor explosives. How else does a big structure get into trouble? I thought about it hard. The Empire State Building—it sways a foot or two at the top; even more in a gale. And that Tacoma bridge; it blew down in—1940, I think. Not one big gust, but a rhythmic series of smaller puffs. Resonance—that's the key. Take a pendulum. You tap it, using maybe ten grams of force. It barely moves. But then you push it again, just at the right time, and it swings in a slightly bigger arc. Keep that up, and in a minute or two, the bob, weighing maybe six or eight ounces, will acquire enough momentum to turn through ninety degrees or more. Like troops marching in step over a long bridge; they could break it down by matching its own period of vibration. Best of all, no insurance trouble. Who would ever try to protect a modern skyscraper against general collapse? The architect would foam at the mouth, he'd be so insulted. Yes, it was the perfect solution—in theory, but hardly practicable at first. I continued to mull it over.

Then I remembered Tesla. Nikola Tesla. He died in 1943, more than eighty years old. Funny how few people can place him. He revolutionized power transmission by high voltage alternating current. He was using radio—and controlling models with it—before Marconi and that bunch knew a crystal from a condenser. Why, he was sending hundred million volt lightning flashes dozens of feet when other scientists were piddling with little two inch sparks. The man was fifty years ahead of his time, and got a dirty deal from history. He was a bigger genius than Edison, Bell, and Westinghouse combined.

Well, Tesla had done some remarkable things with plain, ordinary resonance, too. I suddenly remembered that, and looked up everything available, which isn't much. You see, he kept practically no records, since he was blessed with a mind able to visualize clearly in three dimensions. He could build a new type of dynamo mentally, test it and run it that way, and see every part in operation. When he actually put the machine together, it always worked exactly as he'd expected; the construction was mere routine. That's how he invented the polyphase alternating current system so basic today.

Things were looking up for me now, so I rented an office on the tenth floor of the *Record* building, near the center of percussion, according to my calculations. It was a simple matter to chip away the plaster and concrete of the outside wall, and locate a good, solid steel member. And no office on that side to get suspicious over the noise or vibration—just empty air a hundred feet over the street. Working from my Tesla notes, I built a simple vibrator, using a compact, modern two horsepower electric motor no bigger than a shoebox. It drove a heavy, tough little piston by means of an eccentric cam. I smuggled a lightweight welding outfit into the office with a suitcase, and spot-welded the assembly to the steel girder, using plenty of reinforcing bands as well. I had loads of time, since my office "work" was imaginary. One improvement over Tesla was called for. I put together a neat little electronic feedback unit, using the best transistors available. This device would record the vibrator against the building's motion, and when the period matched, would lock them together for good, so that the amplitude of sway would grow in a hurry.

I wondered whether to include a good battery, but decided that the building's own current ought to do. There was a chance the leads might tear out before the steel frame failed, but I didn't think it too likely. They were heavy, flexible cables, well armored, and should outlast everything else.

When the whole set-up was ready, I filled the rest of the hole in the wall with shredded newspaper—the *Record* itself, too: how's that for a laugh?—and did a professional re-plastering job. All that showed on the outside was a simple switch, just like one for the lights, with a red and black button. Nobody would see it except me and maybe a cleaning woman, and it wouldn't mean a thing to her, although I purposely jammed it during my brief absence from the office.

Well, the building was now at my mercy, but I thought I'd give the *Record* crowd a last chance, so I phoned the editor's office. I finally got him, but when I mentioned my name, and demanded retractions, he got mad and told me not to bother him again, or he'd have me committed to an asylum. Imagine that—as if I were unbalanced or something. Talk about arrogance!

But my conscience was clear, now; he'd had his chance. So back I went to the building last night at seven, when the place was pretty well deserted except for the floor with the presses. The watchman went to my office with me; that's the rule at night—nobody is allowed in the building alone except on the paper's own premises. But, naturally, while he stood outside the door, it was easy to unjam and press the right button, and the first vibrations were hardly apparent a few inches from the wall. Then I brought out the suitcase with the welder and bits of plaster: that was my excuse for going back—the luggage.

If Tesla was right, and I knew damn well he was, my vibrator was soon locked into the correct period, and the building would be swaying a little more each second. In 1896, he had started a tiny vibrator against a beam in his lab, and in a few hours windows were breaking in nearby buildings, and many houses were swaying to the point of collapse. Simple resonance. The police, knowing Nikola, came hotfooting over, and he smashed the thing with a hammer; there wasn't even time to handle it any other way. In a few more minutes half the area might have been in ruins. And that was less than three horsepower at work!

Well, you know the rest; it's all in the papers. The watchman got scared at ten. By that time the swaying was more than obvious, and he thought it was a big temblor. So out he ran, and plenty of the newspaper men followed. The building was rocking like crazy, and the presses were slammed out of true. I see they're a total wreck, which causes me no pain.

But I goofed in one way. I never stopped to think that a new steel building is a lot tougher than the older ones around it. Now the whole area's ready to collapse—the hotels, stores, and houses. Quite a few down already. Nobody knows what's going on except me—and you. They're calling it an earthquake, but that's absurd. Who ever heard of a quake going on for five hours? At increasing magnitude, too. I tell you, Doctor, we've got to stop that vibrator. All you have to do is get the city to stop delivering current in that area. As soon as they do that, the motor will cut out, and everything will go back to normal. Then they can send a crew up to my office and disconnect the whole works.

That's what I was trying to do—get to the master switches in the building, when cops grabbed me and took me here.

Now it's up to you—that's the only way: stop the electricity immediately. If you don't, what with the resonance—don't go; you must believe me. I don't need any shot; tell her to get away from me. Strong arm—that's all you know; I can't fight three interns. If you put me out with that damned needle—you fools! You stupid fools—!

Mulberry Moon

At one end of the laboratory a scintillating light, at first faint and irregular, steadied to a rich, even glow. Walt Tremayne stiffened, and the gas hissed unheeded from the Bunsen burner. As he watched, still holding a flaming match, the intensity increased until the beaker shot a beam of white light to the discolored ceiling.

Elder, gaping over the luminous solution, uttered a choked exclamation: "Walt!"

"God, yes!" Tremayne replied to the unspoken question, reaching mechanically to turn off the gas. "I see it, all right. Be blind not to. Even with all that light coming through the windows. What's going on there, anyway? I thought you were messing with assorted eggs."

"I was—I was. Just using chemicals to start development. My investigation of artificial parthenogenesis. And all of a sudden this thing blossomed under my nose. It's—" He broke off abruptly, stared at his partner, and they cried in almost perfect unison:

"The Army rocket—!"

"That moon rocket offer—!"

They laughed.

"Walt," Elder said, suddenly grave, "I'm not kidding. Just look at that stuff shine. A regular damn searchlight, so help me. Have you ever seen anything like it? I've studied fluorescence in animals; I know all the standard chemicals for producing cold light. I tell you, we've hit on something big."

"Ten thousand bucks." Walt sucked in his breath. "Say, with dough like that we could make a real lab out of this crummy place. A decent centrifuge, not that asthmatic buzz-bomb we've been struggling with."

"Hell with that. You mean a good phase microscope."

"Over my dead body, pal. For that matter, we could spend the whole ten grand on glassware, and still not have enough for both of us." An anxious expression appeared in his eyes. "Sure you can do it again?" he demanded. "Hope you know what was in that beaker."

"Ouch! You are so right. It shouldn't have happened. Kurzin didn't say a word about luminescence—and nobody could miss it." He seized the beaker of still-glowing solution, and studied it. Brows knitted, he dipped a glass rod, and touched it to his tongue. "So that's it," he muttered.

"That's what?" Walt snapped.

"I goofed—but a goof that may give us ten thousand dollars. By mistake I used a beaker with a few drops of ammonium chloride solution in it. That must be what set off the diamino-ortho-phenylazide."

"The what?"

"You heard me. It's a new chemical. Kurzin sent me a few grams from La Jolla last week. Claims it's great stuff for the artificial development of echinoderm eggs. Mighty lucky the old boy didn't get any of his contaminated with an ammonium salt, or our chance at that prize money would be zero minus."

"You mean that's all it takes—ammonium chloride and tongue twister?"

"If my guess is right. And only a one per cent solution, too. Stuff's real potent. Anyhow, we'll soon know—here goes again."

With practiced dexterity the biologist added the chloride to the pink liquid in a liter Erlenmeyer, and the two men waited tensely. Pinpoints of light appeared in the mixture; they coalesced into larger blobs, and within a few seconds a glorious white glow permeated the fluid. They watched it in ecstatic silence.

"Persistent, too," Walt gloated. "See, your first batch is just fading out. Maybe we've solved the whole cold light mystery—licked the fireflies at their own game; wouldn't that be nice?"

"I like that 'we,' " Elder snorted. "Where's the paper? Ah." He flipped the pages. "Here's all the dope. 'Army offers prize for new fluorescent.' " He began to read the lead paragraph aloud, Tremayne peering over his shoulder. " 'A prize of $10,000 in cash has just been offered by the Army for a powerful new fluorescent suitable for use in their moon probe, due to be fired in a few months. It is hoped that such a fluorescent, light in weight, and more effective than any now known, will enable the rocket's arrival to be seen from the Earth. This was not true of the Russian attempt, and success on our part would restore some of the prestige lost. Anybody wishing to submit a new fluorescent for the prize contest may make an appointment with Dr. Joseph Hamilton. If satisfied, he will convene the Technical Committee for a demonstration—' "

"Marshall." Walt tugged at his arm. "Better not get too excited. There could be a lot of work to this before we're ready to ask for an appointment. And we'd better get rolling; there's none too much time."

"All right," Elder said airily. "We'll make the stuff from scratch. Or rather you will. Can you do it? Make Kurzin's compound from the structural formula, all simon pure?"

"I'm a chemist. Anything anybody else can put together, I can, too." He winked. "Especially when they give nice, simple cookbook directions in large type."

"Kurzin says he got the process out of the latest *Journal*. Oh, damn—why did you cancel your subscription?"

"Because I'd rather eat than read the *Journal of Organic Chemistry*," Walt replied in an injured tone. "Unprofessional though it may sound. We'll just borrow Jim Keelyn's copy. Wonder how big a job it is?" He looked about the barren room ruefully. "Will we need any fancy equipment?"

"Better not; that's all I can say," Elder replied sarcastically. "If it can be done with—let me see—two flasks; one cracked; three test tubes, all dirty; and Cavendish's original balance—"

"All right," Tremayne groaned. "Knock it off. We've got things to do. You get that *Journal* from Jim, and I'll start cleaning up this mess in preparation for a little organic synthesis. We'll see what develops."

Out of a black, airless sky the needle pointed rocket fell towards the waiting moon. The last of three stages, it had left the first and second far behind, and now, at a fall from infinity velocity of nearly two miles a second, was about to crash. Inside the gold plated nose cone were twenty-five pounds of the Elder-Tremayne prizewinning fluorescent, just mixed into radiant life by automatic controls. Back on the Earth, trained eyes stared anxiously at the moon's shadowed fraction.

At Palomar the observer left the great Hale telescope puzzled and annoyed. He reported only a faint, momentary glow, and no other observatory was willing to confirm.

"I really think the Army made it this time," he told an assistant. "The telemetering seemed to prove it. But evidently the fluorescent didn't perform as planned. Wonder if they made sure it worked without air. Then again," he added, "if the crust is really a deep layer of pumice, or dust, the nose may have buried itself completely. In that case, no matter how the stuff glowed, we couldn't see it at all. Damned shame. No skin off me, but I hate to see so much dough and months of preparation down the drain." Frowning, he returned to his study of more distant phenomena.

The controversy among the astronomers about the moon's surface was still active a month later, when—

"Walt, did you see this?"

"What?"

"Trenches on the moon! The paper says they're digging trenches on the moon."

"Lay off, will you. Go play with the new centrifuge if you're feeling kittenish. Put your head in it; maybe that'll settle your brains."

"I'm serious," Elder said. "This is no gag. It's right here. All the big scopes have spotted them. Say, what if there *is* intelligent life up there? It can't be so; every biologist knows that; and yet … what would we do if a rocket from some other planet smacked us?"

Walt placed the burette carefully on a clean towel, and turned. "You mean 'they' are afraid of attack—invasion—by us?"

"Sure, why not? First a probe; then a landing by people. Why else would they be digging trenches all of a sudden? They're scared, I'll bet. They've crisscrossed the whole moon with 'em, and the astronomers say they're deepening 'em every day. We ought to reassure the Lunars—or is it Lunatics? Tell 'em we're peaceful—between wars, that is."

"Look," Walt protested. "They can't be trenches. You couldn't see them on the moon. They're only a few feet wide. Be like needle scratches on a medicine ball."

"Sounds reasonable. All I say is, it gives one furiously to think. There must be life up there—intelligent life. If it were Mars, you'd fall back on the big irrigation project; but on the moon—no air, no water, no nothing. It simply doesn't make any sense."

"Let's see the paper," Walt demanded. "Hmmph. Doesn't look like trenches to me. More like a generalized coordinate system—curvilinear coordinates. Or even like a golf ball." He chuckled. "Army honors ex-President-General by turning moon into huge golf ball—what's the matter? You're pale as a sheet."

"Nothing," Elder muttered, the color flooding back to his face. "I was just reminded of something. Does that sketch look to you anything like—well, a mulberry, for example?"

"A mulberry! Man, you really want to top my golf ball, I can see that. Doesn't look like any—yeah, maybe it does, when you hold it like this. It could be some kind of a berry, I suppose. Me, I wouldn't know a mulberry from a farkleberry. You're the farm boy. Anyway, what about it?"

"Nothing," Elder repeated doggedly. "It was just a crazy notion. Too silly to talk about. Forget it. Let's get back to work. I'll give you a hand with the calorimeter while my sections are dehydrating."

"Elder's got a real sourball on," Tremayne was complaining. "Walks around in a daze lately. You can't talk to the guy without getting your head snapped off. Customers are scarce enough for new testing labs without that. Damned if I don't think he's actually worried about the moon invading us over that rocket we sent up at 'em."

Keelyn eyed him gravely. "Is that so impossible?" he drawled. "Plenty of activity up there all of a sudden. Normally they say the moon hardly changes in thousands of years. A tiny new crater appears, or something fades out a little. Now it's fantastic. They must have the whole population at work on a ninety-hour week. Or some incredible earth-moving machinery."

"You, too!" Walt groaned. "That's absurd. Why, nobody's ever even seen a light on the moon. No cities; what the hell kind of a civilization could that be?"

"Owls get along in the dark."

"Oh, for Pete's sake! If you're worried about an invasion by Lunar owls, you can relax. I positively guarantee that our military forces can defeat any number of owls. We are in perfect shape, in spite of a penny pinching government—against owls."

"No; seriously. I just meant that if they can get along without air and water, why not without light? We mustn't try to fit all intelligent life into the one pattern we happen to know about."

"So they live in the dark, maybe underground. But trenches; that's pretty silly. They'd know that trenches would be useless against modern weapons. What'll you bet it turns out to be volcanic activity? Maybe that rocket triggered some instability in the crust."

"What rocket? We can't even be sure it hit. Besides, the moon is battered with meteors all the time. *They* never triggered anything. You haven't explained a thing. Ah, here's Elder—what's your theory, Marshall?"

He glared at them wearily out of reddened eyes. "I don't know," he mumbled, his unshaven face sullen. "But we'll all learn more pretty soon—three weeks, I make it, if the proportion holds."

"What in blazes are you babbling about?" Walt demanded, real concern in his voice. "You all right, Marshall? I still think you ought to see Dr. Lewis—"

"Can it, will you? I'm all right. We'll see who's crazy." He stalked out, muttering.

Keelyn whistled softly. "Say, he *is* bad. When did this start?"

Walt shrugged. "About two weeks ago, I think." He reflected, his brow furrowed; then said uneasily: "I see a little light now. Wonder what's up his sleeve? See this?" He held up the paper. "That headline: 'Science Agog Over Mulberry Moon.' "

"What about it?"

106

"Marshall was jabbering to me about mulberries before these guys saw anything up there but trenches. And that's about the time he began acting so queer. His research has gone to pot, but good. No interest any more."

"Maybe he's unhappy because the fluorescent didn't work. Some of the papers were pretty nasty. Claimed the Army threw away that ten thousand."

"Who says it didn't work?" Walt snapped, bristling. "How do we know the rocket ever got there? Or about the control? Hell, we *know* the stuff works. We've rechecked fifty times."

"Then what's bothering Marshall?"

"I don't know," Tremayne admitted. "But maybe he's on to something the big brains have missed. He's rather lucky that way— look at the fluorescent, for example. I haven't done my duty; too wrapped up in work. I'll get after him tonight. If he knows anything, I'll pry it out if I have to use torture. That's a promise."

There was a derisive sniff, and they whirled, red-faced. Elder stood there, an ironic smile on his lips.

"So you still want my theory, is that it? Okay. But one laugh, and I'll slay you. Don't go, Jim—you might as well certify my insanity, too.

"You're wondering about that mulberry business. Mulberry Moon. Very catchy and alliterative. Do you know the Latin for mulberry? Thought not; you're chemists, barbarians. Well, it's *morula*. School kids learn it, or used to, in freshman science." He chuckled humorlessly.

"What the devil are you getting at?" Walt said. He exchanged uneasy glances with Keelyn. There wasn't much doubt. Marshall was in bad shape.

"We'll see who's nuts," Elder snapped, stung. He wrenched open a thick book, and pointed to a large, graphic sketch. "What does that look like to you?"

"Not a book about it already," Walt marveled.

"Can't you read?" the biologist growled. "It's not a book about 'it' at all. This text has been out for years."

Tremayne gaped at the sketch, reading the caption in complete bewilderment. Then his jaw snapped shut, and he clapped one hand to his head in a theatrical gesture.

"Damn it!" he roared. "You're not suggesting seriously—!"

"Yes, I am!" Elder shouted him down. "What do we know about space, or the moon either, for that matter? All we have to work with is reflected light and a few differential equations of motion. So the moon's a little less dense than the Earth. It's pitted and rough. Well, so is many a fruit-pit, for that matter. What if the surface is this or that mineral—maybe. An oyster shell's calcium carbonate; that's a mineral, isn't it?"

Keelyn made a faint sound of protest deep in his throat. He placed the book gently upon a lab bench.

"Shut up and listen," Elder flashed at him. "I'll hear your objections later. I know 'em all, anyway. I've been making them to myself for days. Now what if millions of years ago, something—and don't ask me what—spread the moon, the asteroids, and even the planets, in the same way a salmon lays eggs? Suppose they never got fertilized?"

"Why not the sun, too?" Walt gulped. "Why so modest?"

"Too hot. Only the cooler bodies. No real proof they ever were very hot. And even if so—well, some crustaceans live in near boiling water. And besides, anything alive has some heat. A hen's egg must be red-hot compared to a stone. Temperature's relative like everything else."

"But the size!" Keelyn protested.

"Hang the size! A Cyclops, so small you need a good lens to see it clearly, lays eggs. So does an ostrich. Or better, so did the Moa. I'll bet a Moa's egg is just as large in relation to a Cyclops' egg as the moon is to a Moa's egg. Anyway, you get my point."

Walt said: "How could anything live in space for millions of years? The cold; lack of oxygen, and—"

"Don't make me laugh. Anthrax spores will lie in the ground fifty years, winter and summer, and after being boiled for an hour, wipe out a herd of cattle. Just give them the right environment and a little time. That's all it takes."

"But the moon's not getting any bigger."

"Why should it? You're thinking of certain kinds of eggs. Did you ever watch a frog's egg develop? It doesn't change in bulk, at least not to any extent. Same with many insect eggs. All you see are cleavage lines deepening, and when the grub appears, it's roughly the size of the egg itself."

"So when *this* hatches—?"

"Yes," Elder said grimly. "Only moon size; no larger." He brushed back a strand of hair with fingers that shook. "At first."

"If I understand you," Walt said, "you're actually implying that our fluorescent started that—that egg developing."

"You bet it did. You saw how those starfish eggs reacted to the most dilute solution. No milt ever did any better."

"So that's why there was no flash. The crust was soft, and the rocket punched right in."

"Exactly. Like pin-pricking an egg to start development."

"There's no proof," Keelyn said weakly. "It's all speculation."

"Proof's coming," was Elder's reply. He reached for the biology text. "The next stage—" He turned the page. "There it is."

They looked at the sketch, then at each other, and were silent.

(Extract From the Diary of James Keelyn)

Marshall was right. The thing has reached the blastula stage, and much faster than predicted, although the concave portion is still small and shallow.

Walt and Marshall have stopped clowning; in a way that's very significant to anyone who knows them. They are preparing a summary of the facts, which they plan to present privately to certain top scientists and government officials. They are not hopeful about it. What can Earth do? The rocket took many months to prepare, and even with a hydrogen warhead would be too small for the job.

Already the quality of moonlight has changed. It has a purplish tinge, and for some reason—is it the roughening of the surface?—is much dimmer. Do they still make love under this ghastly moon?

I wonder if the thing might not abort. Maybe after so many millions of frozen, airless years, it will fail to mature, remaining in the blastula or gastrula stage. But Marshall showed us anthrax spores under the microscope. They shone brightly, so much like tiny moons themselves. He has it right—as far as anybody knows these spores could resume their active state after a thousand years.

No, it will not abort. The vitality of so many years is not easily destroyed.

What Behemoth will hatch from that devil's egg? Will it spread monstrous, utterly impossible wings, and flap off into space? Or will it prowl the solar system as a beast of prey prowls the feeding ground of its birth?

The Melanas

"I reject the whole idea. You'll never convince me this is right." Caslor's dark eyes were brooding; his taught, eager face unusually grim. "There's no real necessity for mass destruction, or indeed for any killing."

"So you've said—and have been repeating for weeks now," Partol replied, wearily good humored. "But you don't really offer any evidence to support the 'anti's.' "

Caslor frowned, leaning forward, his slight body tense. "I haven't any. Not that practical people would accept. Call it intuition, a hunch, if you like, but I urge, I beg—do not begin such a bloody campaign against these harmless animals."

"You don't understand the problem." Partol's smile was indulgent. "You're neither a scientist nor a farmer—only a poet. No, don't take offense," he added quickly, as Caslor flushed in resentment. "I retract the 'only.' Nobody appreciates your art more than I, believe me. But we're dealing with a practical question, a nasty, unpoetic one, that must be faced in a realistic way. Think of it like this. Here we are, living on the most beautiful planet that ever circled a star. Just look." He gestured towards the open window. From their sunny perch in the topmost chamber of a sky-flung crystal-wood tower, they could see mile after mile of lush, green meadows, varied with stands of mighty trees, and wearing great concourses of glowing flowers proudly, like medals on the breast of a reclining hero.

A group of children, shrieking joyously, raced over the springy turf; and a flock of scarlet birds rose before them like living fireworks. Their melodic chirping, like distant bells, made fairy music. A fragrant breeze stirred the room's gay tapestries; it held the scent of spring in its cool threads. Caslor's melancholy eyes brightened momentarily. He had seen thirty springs, each more nearly perfect than the last. Partol was right; their world was incomparable.

"On this whole planet," Partol resumed, "there is not a single dangerous animal—nothing that bites, or claws, or stings. No carnivores at all. And only one living thing that can be called obnoxious."

"But it's not," Caslor protested. "People are blind, convinced of something utterly false. There is a strange restlessness tormenting them."

"True," Partol admitted thoughtfully. "There has been some recognition of that fact. Farmers have grumbled about *melanas* for centuries, yet only now does any action seem really imminent. I have never seen people so stirred up. Still, why fight the torrent? What do these animals matter, after all? They might not be objectionable in any less perfect environment; I concede that. And they're probably pretty little brutes, physically, judging, of course, from the scantiest evidence. But they're nuisances all the same. There's not a valley that isn't overrun with them, and they destroy a large percentage of our crops. That's their main sin. In addition—and this bothers me more, since I'm not a farmer—they call constantly in those nerve-wracking squeaks. Did you ever notice, incidentally, that the more beautiful the surroundings, the more of these wretched beasts congregate there, spoiling the perfection with their unholy racket? They remind me of a false note in a great symphony—or a wrong word in a fine poem. If you found such a word in your sonnet, wouldn't you remove it?"

"If I did, it would be to put a better one in its place. Would a blank be any better? Besides, there is an old theory—a superstition, I admit—that the Gods resent perfection. Do not take folklore, old racial taboos, too lightly; historians have learned that."

"You are eloquent today," Partol said, giving him a wondering glance.

"Words are my profession," was the bitter reply. "That is why the men of action have swept me aside in this controversy. Not that action has been our forte in the past. We are a strangely introspective people, and have fathered many queer doctrines. Have you ever considered our peculiar penchant for fantasy—or hallucination, if you prefer? It pervades all our literature and painting."

Partol nodded. "It is quite true that we are basically a sensitive, gentle race, simple in our tastes and habits. We are satisfied with our crops and plain houses, having no advanced technology, nor feeling the need of one. But a civilization cannot remain static indefinitely, even in a perfect environment. It must advance or retreat; and many of us now feel it is time to expand—to realize fully our potentialities. At least, that is one reason given by those who most strongly urge this—this extermination."

"Fulfillment by pointless slaughter?"

Partol shrugged. "Their first step, strange though it might seem to you, is the extirpation of these melanas. If nothing else, this campaign should prove a yardstick of our abilities. To wipe out such elusive, alert animals will be a first class intelligence test. And it will teach us the power of concerted action, of unity of purpose. There is too much individualism among us for real progress. This will toughen our fiber as a race. Or so the argument goes," he added, as if a little unsure of his own reasoning.

"How will you manage it?" Caslor asked, his voice cold. "We've had no weapons for years—no traps, no poisons. There are no records of such horrors after the First People, thousands of years ago."

"The Council meets today, remember. Why not sit in and hear for yourself? Darkon surely will have a solution. His committee has been at work for weeks."

"I'll be there. Maybe one more appeal will stop this senseless project. Has anybody ever found a dead melana?" he queried with apparent irrelevance.

"I don't know. What difference does that make?" Partol replied, puzzled. "You're always talking in riddles." His tone was mildly reproving, but his hand was on Caslor's shoulder as they walked out.

The Council meeting was the most remarkable within the memory of the oldest members. Ordinarily the uncomplicated lives of the people were reflected in the casual, direct decisions of their representatives. Occasionally agricultural land was released to the flaming wildflowers that sprang up so quickly, housing new melana colonies almost as fast. A few seasons of flowering, and the soil acquired new fertility for food plants. More rarely a community farm asked for and received permission to expand. Once in decades a controversy between two of the sleepy, isolated towns was resolved without unseemly squabbling by calm elders of the Council.

But today the air crackled with emotional static. It may have been only that the prospect of planet-wide action, something wholly new and exciting, was before them; or that somehow a radical, stimulating ideology had taken hold of a gentle people whose normal instincts would have rejected it with abhorrence. Even the most stolid felt uneasy, and squirmed in their seats.

"Last time we met," the President reminded them gravely, "it was the Council's decision to exterminate the melanas if possible. This step was not taken lightly; all of us detest killing, and we have never before in our history found it necessary.

"Evidence against this expedient was presented by Caslor, as well as others, and was respectfully heard. But our verdict was given and recorded. Today, therefore, we are ready for proposals about implementing that decision." He concluded with the traditional formula: "Who will speak?"

"I will speak." Caslor stood defiantly erect.

"Speak, Caslor," the President said courteously.

"I beg the Council to reverse this decision. Such a request is, I know, unprecedented, but so is the order itself. Why are the melanas being destroyed? Think of the flimsy reasons—pretexts, really—and draw back for shame. Because they nibble a little of our crops! Do our children starve? Does any ever go hungry in all the world?

"Because they squeak! What you hold to be so discordant is only strange, different, wonderful. I have listened to melanas since I was a child, and now I will tell you a great truth lately come to me. The melana sings! Yes, sings in a glorious, complex, 36-note scale. Listen with the heart; delight will follow. My friends, hear me. There is much that is odd and mysterious about these phantom animals. Their hymn to the rising sun may prove to be one of the most precious heritages of our ancient race. They have lived here unmolested longer than we; our oldest records mention them. Who knows what delicate balance of nature may be upset by our heedless meddling? Why is it that every great artist has been abnormally sensitive to these creatures?

"I repeat: do not exterminate the melanas!" He sat down, his face stony.

"I will speak!" A blocky, ruddy little man was on his feet.

"Speak, Forban," said the President.

"Caslor refers lightly to crop damage. Farmers are not so casual. One-tenth is the toll taken. One-tenth, think of it! Surely we would pay even that, and gladly, were there any proper return. We have no wish to kill wantonly. But what good is a melana to anybody? Alive or dead, he is never seen, except by the keenest eyes, and then only as a vague, furtive form gliding among the flowers. If he has beauty, who enjoys it? The *faltur* birds and the golden *delmines* we can see, and love. Nobody would harm them. The melana's weird cries annoy us; they are not musical, like the *silidor*. Caslor says they sing, but who else in all the world has ears for such melody?

"Yes, and further, it is well known that he who lingers too long near a colony suffers terrible headaches, faulty vision, and strange delusions, even to the point of madness. It is quite possible that they poison the air in some way. Many of the farmers fear them, and cannot work well when they are about. Consider this, too, as against Caslor: why is it that the loveliest flower-vales always have the most of these pestilential beasts?

"I say to you: there is no room on our planet for the melana!"

"And I warn you—all of you," Caslor cried in exasperation. "You know nothing of killing. I have never slain, but I can see through other eyes than those of experience. Killing is a madness, and he who kills will never be quite sane again. The death of an individual may at times be beautiful, but not slaughter!"

"Might not crops be protected by fences?" Partol suggested diffidently to Forban.

"That was tried," he retorted. "A hundred or more years ago. The melanas always get through. Not even metal keeps them out, and there is not enough of it for such use, anyhow. Over, under, or around, they reach our crops."

"I must remind the Council," the President said mildly, "that our decision is taken. We can consider methods only. Who will speak?"

"I will speak." Darkon, the tall, cool biologist arose, turning his back to Caslor. "My committee has studied the melana. There is much of interest, yet facts are scarce. Little is known of their structure. Dead melanas are never found. But this is not so strange as some think. We have not killed any, and those dying of natural causes—if indeed they ever die—are doubtless carried off by their companions. We need not fear upsetting the balance of nature, regardless of Caslor. Nothing feeds on the melana; they eat only our crops. It follows that to remove them affects only one phase of our ecology. Without melanas, no other organism will perish, since none depends on them. And our crops will increase by a tenth. It is as simple as that.

"From ancient records we have garnered a few impressionistic sketches. It appears that our ancestors, incredibly patient and sharp-eyed, saw melanas quite often. They tended to regard it as sacred. From the most scanty evidence, therefore, we may be certain only that the beast is small, of fragile structure, very quick moving, and extremely wary.

"Now, as to the method of destruction, one fact is the key. Melanas always gather in the flower-valleys by day. There is no record of this peculiar behavior pattern ever varying. At night, of course, as farmers know all too well, the melanas leave these valleys to nibble crops; but they never fail to return to their own colonies by sunrise.

"A number of possible weapons were suggested by committee members, mostly based on those of the First People. But we must remember our unfamiliarity with such devices. There would be great danger of killing or maiming each other, especially at close quarters. Therefore, we recommend a more primitive, but safer method.

"Let a thousand men, preferably those skilled in the game of *slakmak*, which, as you all know, employs a club-like implement against a small ovoid, be chosen for this task. Each morning a flower-vale will be surrounded by a circle of armed, active men. They will close in, permitting no melanas to get by, even should any try to leave their valley, something highly unlikely. In this manner, all the animals can be clubbed to death with slakmat bats, and none missed. Since the bat is well padded, there is little danger of our being injured."

A faint murmur of disapproval rippled through the Council, and the President said distastefully: "Is there no less brutal way?"

Darkon shrugged. "I can think of none. Weapons are too dangerous in unpracticed hands; and we know nothing of melana physiology even if we cared to prepare poison. Besides, such poison might kill other, useful animals. The bats are familiar toys to thousands."

"How long will it take?"

"Perhaps six months. With ten thousand men, we could finish very quickly, but use of so many might disrupt our economy. We cannot fail to destroy them all, since they are instinctively barred, it would seem, from leaving their colonies by day. If they scattered to the cultivated areas, the problem would be much more difficult."

The President sighed. After a moment he said reluctantly: "Let us vote on Darkon's proposal."

One by one a majority of the elders nodded their consent. Outside, a crowd of farmers roared approval as word of the decision reached them. Caslor sneered whitely at their cheering.

"You needn't participate," Partol consoled him. "Even if by some ill chance you are chosen, you can get excused."

A wry smile twisted Caslor's lips. "Certainly I would refuse to kill. But I must be there at the last. There is a riddle to be read, and if I can find the solution in time … I pray that I can. Yet I feel a terrible dread. There is something all wrong, Partol; I can sense it hovering about like a fog of evil and stupidity. The Council should have resisted this transient mood of our people; in time it would pass away. Now it may be too late to save us from—from what?"

Partol eyed him glumly. "At least, your hands will be clean, whatever happens."

"You are wrong; all of us share this collective guilt."

In silence they left the Council Chamber.

Five months had passed, and they stood with their fellows before a valley carpeted with fiery blooms. A thin line of scarlet flowers made a bloody flash down the center of a wide, yellow patch.

"The very last colony," Partol said. "A month ahead of schedule." He glanced compassionately at Caslor's thin, ravaged face. "I assure you, I'm sorry I was picked. Of course, it was Darkon's spite—an attempt to hurt you. But had I realized the messiness of clubbing these little creatures, I would have paid the heavy fine instead. No wonder there were never any bodies found; a dead melana evaporates—what is the technical word?—sublimes, that's it. Like a puff of perfume. It is so much better than cremation.

"The most horrible aspect of the whole thing—and you predicted it—is the way this slaughter has corrupted the people. Their faces are frightening. Well, here we go; the ring is forming. I shall never enjoy a slakmak game again, I fear. What's the matter?"

"Does your head ache at these killings?" Caslor asked haltingly.

Partol grimaced. "Yes," he admitted. "I hesitated to mention it. I abhor superstition. But all the farmers in our group discuss it freely. Double vision, too, at times. Perhaps, as they said, the vapors of the dead melanas are poisonous. Or maybe just the power of suggestion. You must admit that your other fears were baseless; there has been no catastrophe, after all."

"You will never be sane again," Caslor said in a low voice. "You have killed wantonly. That is one catastrophe. And yet the riddle—"

"Don't worry about me," Partol answered grimly. "But you—why do you torture yourself watching?"

"I hoped to find a clue in time." After a pause, he added in a plaintive, childlike voice: "Partol, does it seem to you as if the grass and flowers danced oddly just then?"

"Too busy to notice," the other grunted, as he moved with the closing circle of clubbers. "Heat waves, probably. How they squeak! My head is splitting."

"It's a dirge. Why does the landscape out there look so drab? Wasn't a cluster of trees standing on the hill a moment ago? Those few melanas in the center must be the last in the world. Can't they be spared? Those bloody clubs ... I—" He broke off, his face grey and flaccid. "Partol, Partol—the riddle! I've solved it! Stop them—they must stop!"

He thrust through the tightening ring. Many men were standing aside, leaning wearily on bloodstained clubs. Before them tiny, battered bodies, golden and furry, were subliming into puffs of perfumed, faintly colored gasses. Even the fluids on the bats vanished quickly.

But a small group of men still moved in relentlessly on the vibrating grass blades that marked a last pocket of melanas. For a few seconds the frenzied poet made progress, but now he plunged in vain against the inner ring, shouting, pleading, his face wet with perspiration. Glazed eyes, mechanically flailing arms, features of cold metal—these men were beyond reach of his revelation. A thick hand hurled him back, a vicious blow that flung his gaunt body to one knee. He knelt there, weeping angry tears.

A single wailing cry rang thinly, futilely over the valley, which was dislimning like a dream. As it died out, there vanished also, one by one, like candle flames in a chill wind, the last green fields, the last towering trees, the last glowing flowers. Caslor stared about, dazed and terrified; for out to the misty horizon there remained but the world's naked core: raw rock, seamed and ugly, a lump of slag fit only for the ash heap of the universe.

A Civilized Community

He was quite alone, X million miles from home, on the wrong planet; even the order of X was unknown. M'lu could not see the stars in daylight, but had no doubt they would be unfamiliar. Perhaps this was even another universe.

The experimental ship, designed to test the new space warp, had somehow malfunctioned. Instead of emerging only a few parsecs at most from their moon base, they had flashed back to normal drive right inside the atmosphere of a strange planet in who knows what galaxy. Despite every effort of the skilled pilot, backed by all his wonderful instruments, the ship was not built to take such a strain. Torn and pitted by a searing plasma of heavy gasses, the vessel had crashed. M'lu was the only survivor, a near miracle for which a post in the stern and the accident of extra thick plates on his back and belly were responsible. Even so, three of his twelve legs were dangling uselessly, and he sensed many internal injuries as well.

It was fortunate, of course, that the atmosphere of the strange planet could sustain his respiration; less encouraging was its gravitational field, which he felt to be at least double the one at home. But to a strong, low slung animal like M'lu, his weight was not too severe a handicap.

Of all the members of that carefully selected crew, he was perhaps the least fitted to battle an alien environment. M'lu was a mathematical physicist, knowing little of biology, and even less of violence. His race was a gentle, philosophical one, respectful of all life, but without any mawkish sentimentality. At home, although theirs was the dominant species, because of high intelligence and an exploding technology, they had preserved most of the planet's other lifeforms, which were, on the whole, attractive and harmless.

M'lu had no exaggerated fear of death, but he enjoyed being alive, and believed strongly in the great community of intelligence. If there was rational life on this world, he would try hard to find it. He would never be able to return home; that was obvious. Even though he could design another ship, how could he trust the space warp mechanism now? And how could he find his own solar system in some distant galaxy? No, it was clear that he must live out his life here, and that was a prospect bearable only if other minds, approximately equal to his own, were available for communion.

All that he had left of his personal equipment was on the harness he wore: some mementos of home and family, and the handgun. The few heavy weapons were lost when the ship burned; only a part of the stern was intact, and it held nothing of value to him now.

The ground here was rolling and gentle, with patches of thick vegetation. M'lu cast his thoughts out in a wide net, hoping to reach a sympathetic mind, but there was no response. Nor could he see any sign of civilization. This was discouraging, but not final. Some species do not project their thoughts as far as others; at home, a few kinds of animals even communicated by means of sounds. In any case, individual, primitive creatures could not help him much; M'lu sought a city, or at least a village—some community of rational, social beings who would feed and nurse him.

So, with his crippled legs dangling—fortunately, they were not all on the same side—he moved through the tangled growths in the spiral, searching path which his mathematical training told him was best suited to the situation.

Although he proceeded with caution, M'lu was unprepared, psychologically, for this environment. There had been no briefing in his case, since he had been expected to function only as chief engineer on a test flight. Many of his companions, who had participated in colonizing flights near their own planet, would have known just what to do; but M'lu did not have the background. Before he had gone more than a few yards, the alien was under savage attack. Red, jointed animals, roving in an apparently aimless way, closed in on the bewildered M'lu. They seized several of his legs in their powerful little jaws, immobilizing them; others tried to gnaw through his armor.

He tore the creatures off with his own four anterior appendages, amazed at the strength of their hard bodies. But dozens of others boiled out of a black hole in the ground, swarming over him. His thick plates saved him from serious injury, but already they were forcing him in a direction he didn't like—the opening of their underground nest. Once dragged down into that gloomy cavern, M'lu knew there would be no returning.

Once more he hurled his thoughts out to the red beasts: "I come in peace. Help me." But there was no reaction. He could sense their individual auras of consciousness, but the ranges were pitifully short, the egos redly savage, the thoughts inchoate and blurred. There was no intelligence there to accept his friendly overtures.

Reluctantly, M'lu decided it was time for stronger measures. He pulled the handgun from his harness, adjusted the blast radius, and fired into the pack. Fifteen of the attackers collapsed, their legs twitching aimlessly. Two more well placed discharges, and he was almost free. M'lu ripped away the last three brutes that clung to him, and fled. His nine good legs bore him away at a speed the red beasts couldn't match; soon he was out of their territory.

But it had been an exhausting fight; M'lu needed food badly. He tried, in a gingerly way, some of the more tempting plants, but their acrid juices burned his sensitive gullet, used to the nectars of his home planet. Finally, after sampling a dozen different types with no luck, he gave up. He would have to hold out until safe in a community; there, the scientists could confer with him, and no doubt find suitable food, or else synthesize some, if necessary.

So far, however, there was not the slightest sign of civilization; just strange beasts, predators, probably, roaming about. They didn't respond to his thoughts; and many looked very formidable in appearance, so that he was afraid to approach them. So he listened for their short range, primitive thought patterns, and avoided as many as he could. But the second attack, when it came, was from an unexpected direction.

M'lu had been resting in the shade of a rocky outcrop, when something huge fluttered down right out of the sky, stabbing at him with a long, horny mouth. It was a black animal, much bigger than he, a biped with beady, malicious eyes. A host of smaller things clung to its shiny body; M'lu could see them plainly, and wondered at their likeness, in miniature, to himself.

But there was no time to think at them, or to speculate, either. The sharp bill drove for his midsection, and M'lu rolled aside just in time, every joint of his long body quivering. In spite of his increased weight, he was still fast, so that the horny spear only scraped the tough plates of one side. M'lu snatched at the handgun; there was no time to narrow its beam to a more effective width, so he fired at the diffuse setting used on the red animals. He aimed squarely at the thing's head, aware of the great ganglion there, and he held the stud down, since the brute was large and powerful.

The creature gave a hoarse squawk of agony, and danced about, its jet wings trailing. It fell to one side, and a gleaming red drop appeared at the tip of its bill. Then, with a mighty flapping, it staggered into the air and flew off, calling harshly. A number of others joined it in the air; the whole flock circled about it, echoing its cries. M'lu hid in a hollow under the rock until they were gone.

Only then did he realize that the black animal's thought aura had been both stronger and more meaningful than those of the red beasts. But he knew there was still insufficient intelligence there for his needs—just vague images of food and sudden pain.

That last prolonged shot had finished the energy store of the handgun; it was doubtful if any punch was left. Those who had fitted out the ship had not counted on anything like this. The crew was supposed to test the space warp, then return. M'lu had kept this one weapon in a locker, until the captain told him regulations required each crew member to wear it in space. Odd that a master going by rulebook, with no suspicion of trouble, should have done M'lu such a good turn, entirely by accident. The handgun had saved his life twice now, but wasn't likely to be of much help again. To kill or disable animals as large and fierce as these took the heaviest charges. M'lu sighed, and doggedly plowed ahead, fighting his way through tangled plant stems tougher and more rubbery than anything at home.

Oh, for a city! A group of rational beings who worked together, communicated freely, and had some kind of culture worthy of the name.

It was late in the day now; before too long that great yellow sun would be setting. M'lu was worried about the night. Without food and medical care, he might not survive the hours of darkness, even if the wild beasts left him alone.

As he moved along, the vegetation thinned out; then, under his feet was a kind of paving that raised his hopes to new heights. Undoubtedly this dark, resinous stuff was the work of intelligent beings; people with an advanced technology. The community he sought must surely be close, now.

M'lu increased his speed, nine sturdy legs working like pistons. Every few minutes he flung out his waves of thought, hoping to encounter a receptive mind. Nothing; still nothing. But perhaps the creatures had a short range; that didn't necessarily mean a low intelligence. But it would be so reassuring to receive a thought—one diamond-hard, clear, glowing thought—from out there.

Even as he made this silent plea, another wild beast, this one clothed in a furry hide, sprang upon M'lu, snapping at his plates with white teeth like chips of glass. The animal had a ferocity that was appalling; none of the previous attacks had been so well coordinated and fast.

M'lu grabbed for the handgun, hoping to squeeze a last small charge from the weapon, but it was knocked from his grasp. The creature outweighed him, and seemed to be composed of steel springs; but M'lu was no weakling, even in his injured condition, and he was desperate. But his chief advantage was one of reason. Four anterior appendages, with their strong fingers and two thumbs, kept the gnashing jaws from his body. The animal had talons on all four feet, but they were blunt, so M'lu ignored them for the moment, although they tore at his armor in a scrabbling motion.

Acting with blinding speed, he then released two of the wiry fingers to jab at the beast's eyes. Even as he did so, M'lu felt a wry wonder at his own brutality; never would he have dreamed himself capable of deliberately gouging the eyes of any living thing.

But it had to be; the fingers stabbed home above the narrow, quivering snout, and the furry animal squeaked in pain. M'lu tore free, expecting a renewed attack, but the alien beast was thrashing about in fear and bewilderment, its world forever darkened. Hastily, M'lu circled the struggling brute, and hurried past. In this cruel environment, he reflected, a blind animal can't live long; some other thing will surely kill it before dark. What a tragedy to be born on such a planet!

But then, as he rounded a turn in the dark path, just as the sun was setting, M'lu felt like flinging out a constellation of joyful thoughts. A city—no, a small village, actually—but for all that a community of civilized beings. There could be no doubt. Just a few yards away was the first house, built of wood, and set high on a pillar. Wood was a rather primitive building material, but M'lu's own ancestors had once used it, and they had been well advanced even then.

M'lu sent out an urgent thought; it flew ahead past all the ranked houses; there were more than fifty. And still no reply came winging back. No matter. Short range or not, this was a community of rational beings. Those huge wooden houses, each big enough for many families, were held together with metal pegs, he saw; moreover they were coated with some kind of plastic material as a protection against the elements. Such techniques meant a highly developed culture.

Well, if they couldn't receive his thoughts at this distance, M'lu would go to them. He hurried to the nearest pillar, and tried again. No doubt there was either an elevator inside, or perhaps a winding stair. No, that was too advanced. Probably they dropped a ladder, or a basket at the end of a rope. He hurled more thoughts, and then, in despair, made snapping noises with his mandibles. Finally, he even produced a thin, wailing cry from his respiratory organs. No response from above; nobody came from the house to the platform to look at him.

It was almost dark now; no wonder people lived up on such pillars; it was a simple but effective way to baffle the feral animals of this harsh world.

M'lu was not a master climber, but the wood was rough, and his nine good legs well equipped with claws, pads, and clinging hairs. As he worked his way up to the platform, he heard a reassuring sound: electrical machinery at work. That meant a first rate technology. Soon he would have help.

He scrambled wearily over the edge of the flat, wooden flooring, and lay there resting for a moment. The entrance to this house was a circular opening in the thick boards. Obviously it had been done with a power tool, electrical, of course. He crawled to the hole, and went in. What was this? No light? The time of rest so early? Why not; this wasn't home, after all.

He began to broadcast again: "Help me! I come in peace; I am badly hurt. Help me!"

And there he died, one more alien in a society that tolerates very few. They killed him with their poisoned daggers, skillfully finding the joints in his armor. He died without knowing that only a few hundred yards away was a mind almost the equal of his own; one that hungered for communication. But the citizens destroyed M'lu. They had a complex language, but it was not his; and no alien that enters the City of the Bees may live.

In the house, Luther Galbraith, a PhD in Physics from Cal Tech, suddenly stiffened in his chair as something seemed to explode in the fabric of his brain. His wife, hearing a moaning cry, hurried in from the kitchen. She saw his white face, and gasped: "What is it? What's wrong?"

"Did you hear anything?" he demanded.

"No, of course not—except you. It scared me to death. What made you groan like that?"

He put his hands to his head; they were shaking.

"I thought I heard a terrible scream—like something dying. But it was inside my head."

They stared at each other in silence.

Outside, in one of the fifty hives, the bees' sanitary corps flung M'lu's body to the earth below the platform.

Alien

He was born in a strange way, having neither a father nor mother, nor even any ancestors. One moment he was not, and the next, a miracle of consciousness had occurred.

At first he was aware only of warmth and wellbeing; he possessed neither sight nor hearing, but merely a vague tactile sense. About him flowed an ocean of sensations, but almost all of it was beyond his ken. He was aware that other living things were moving around him, but their nature remained obscure.

He grew rapidly, and with the increase in bulk came greater consciousness. The heat was always more pleasant; the nourishment a delight to his being; and life itself a kind of continuing ecstasy, without a single flaw.

Finally came thought, and communion with his own kind. He had no mobility, but didn't miss it, because the world moved past his body ceaselessly, bringing new warmth, fresh food, and vital oxygen. To exchange thoughts with others like himself was merely a final boon, the ultimate gift of a kindly universe.

He was gentle in spirit; never having experienced either hunger or cruelty, pain or fear, he felt nothing but good will toward all life.

As his mind gained power, he was able to commune with more distant members of his race. They were essentially poets and philosophers, having no knowledge of science. This was an inevitable consequence of their physical structure: lacking mobility and appendages, experiment, the lifeblood of science, was not for them.

But they ranged widely, and to great depths, in pure mathematics, and spun endless philosophical theories about the universe. They were placid, poetic, benevolent, and almost fearless. Almost, but not quite, for their world did have one flaw, a single great mystery.

As he grew to be a giant of his species, he tended to concentrate on this unique problem, questioning all of his communicants in detail, but the information was scanty and inconsistent.

"What happens when one of us suddenly drops from the skein of thought?" That was the key question he repeatedly hurled at his elders. "Tell me about every such case you know."

They gave him all the data they had, and he spent many long hours pondering the facts, and attempting to classify them. It soon became apparent that such disappearances fell into a limited number of categories.

The oldest of these, handed on as a tradition from one generation to another, was also the least frightening. A member of the community would suddenly complain: "The food is bad. I'm getting cold." His plaints would become more urgent, his messages vague and incoherent. Then, in a relatively short time, his voice would fade out forever.

The second category was much more puzzling, and provoked greater apprehension. A communicant would report his universe gone wild. His stream of nourishment would become sour, as if full of poison, a strange and terrible sensation would envelop his whole being, and finally, most incomprehensible of all, he would be torn from his fixed spot in the universe. After that, the lines of communication invariably were broken.

The third aspect of the great mystery was equally terrifying. Suddenly, with no warning, an awful light might stream into the world. Sometimes it came from only one direction; often it drove in from all sides. In either case it struck the tender bodies with millions of deadly lances, shriveling and destroying in a cataract of pain. Once that intolerable ordeal began, no member of the community uttered a single coherent thought—only mad screams that made its fellows exchange wondering queries.

Another phase of the final mystery was rather similar. In this case, you were aware of a foreign body thrust into your own. It hissed and sparkled in a peculiar way, and the scintillating light it shed destroyed everything around it. Here, too, communication soon broke down, the victim quickly becoming incoherent.

It was a mighty mystery, and worthy of much thought. But it didn't change his nature significantly, because it was only hearsay. To be cruel, one must suffer cruelty. To fear pain, one must experience it; and in their world, the experience was also the end; there was no reprise.

And always he grew, drinking the warm, tasty food, feeling his body expand, glorying in the strength of his mind. It was a world without sex, and yet every change in bulk was accompanied by hundreds of tiny thrills that were sexual in their impact.

As he increased in size, his good will and benevolence grew, too. The poems he made, and shared with his kind, were models of unswerving love. Even his mathematics underwent a change. It was mathematics without any physical referents, of course; bloodless stuff involving pure numbers. "Find three squares in arithmetical progression," was a favorite that he proposed.

About this time, he discovered one more fact about the last mystery—a disquieting bit of evidence. By comparing a great many reports from the elders, he hit upon a new generalization: the faster you grew, the shorter time you remained in communication. A member of the species had once grown very slowly, and lasted fifty years, an almost incredible record. Others, attaining equal or greater bulks in fewer months, were lost in less than a year.

He was three years old, and the largest of all the communicants. Nobody had ever raised the question: Was it possible to stop growing? He began to experiment, but found it was beyond his control. Although his mind was a tight unit, it didn't rule the physical world of his body; the parts had autonomy. This discovery was very interesting to his friends; many philosophical theories were invented to explain it.

One more year, he grew: the kindly, benevolent, vastly learned leader of the tribe, loved and respected by all.

Then the great mystery opened to him.

A strange sourness pervaded his food; the sweet liquid turned rancid, so that he rejected it. A little later, from somewhere above, came a flood of light; to him it was just sensation, but new and unpleasant.

And finally, he knew both pain and fear, as great gleaming tongs tore him from his fixed point in the center of the universe. There were no more benevolent thoughts; just wild screams, incoherent and insane. Then the lines were down.

The surgeon held the flaccid, dripping mass up so the medical students could see it.

"The worst kind," he said grimly. "Malignant as they come." He dropped the tumor in the slop basin.

Irresistible Attraction

"A *grif* has been after the vegetables," the Gardener reported. "Tomatoes and carrots were taken away."

"That is surprising," said the Custodian. "It has been a long time since any grifs were seen around here. This must be stopped at once. The Master's crops are for Him alone."

"He has been gone for many seasons now. Maybe He will never return."

"That is a forbidden thought, like others of yours lately. You have been badly instructed. I never get such ideas, nor do my assistants. No matter how long the Master is away, He will come back; and we must account for every year's harvest."

"But already the warehouses bulge," the Gardener persisted. "After this season there will be no more storage space."

"That is not our problem. The Estate Manager will build more granaries."

"I don't see why the Master may eat, and yet it is wrong for a grif to get hungry."

"The Masters own this world. They took it over long before you or I knew about anything. It is not for us to question. Especially you, who are only a gardener, knowing just enough to till the soil."

"That is true," the other admitted, without resentment. "My job is to make things grow. Lettuce, cabbage, potatoes, fruit—I bring them from the ground."

"How did the grif get in?"

"There is a tunnel under the fence. It must be a cunning beast, this one."

"Grifs are relatively intelligent. They degenerated from a position of dominance. In the old days, before you served the Master, there was a nest of grifs in the foothills. They gave us much trouble until we trapped and poisoned them. The grif is dying out. There cannot be more than a hundred on the whole planet. Well, I shall have to do something about this one. If it has young, the family could spoil a lot of food in a year. The Master will be very angry if his harvests are damaged or carried off."

"There is more food in the warehouse than He could eat in a hundred years. After all, He has no family."

"You don't understand these matters. Stick to your spraying and fertilizing. Let me deal with the grif."

"And just how will you do that?"

"I'm not sure," the Custodian admitted. "In those days, it wasn't my problem, so I didn't pay close attention. It seems to me that traps were most effective. Although we can see in the dark, and grifs cannot, they can hear us from some distance off. Our weight doesn't make for stealth. Except for that, flame-guns would be the answer."

"Where will you get traps?"

"They are stored somewhere. I shall find them and place a few near the tunnel. Grifs are cunning, but do not understand mechanisms. If anything hums, or flashes, or smells of ozone, they seem able to detect it very quickly, and flee. Machines terrify them; that is why simple traps are probably best. No hunter with a gun can get close enough; and even if one lies in wait, a grif senses danger and stays out of range. We may feel that no animal can spot us, but there must be something to give us away. But leave the matter to me. I'll get your grif. Now better get back to your vegetables."

"Very well, Custodian." The Gardener left.

After examining the master inventory of the estate, the Custodian found a set of traps in Warehouse 6. They were in excellent condition after fifteen years, and needed only to be energized and supplied with fresh poison. He brought two of them to where the Gardener was spraying tomatoes.

"I have the traps. Show me the grif's tunnel. I hope you didn't fill it."

"Of course not. It is just beyond the peach orchard." He led the Custodian through the magnificent stand of flawless fruit trees to where an untidy pile of dark subsoil bulked against the high wire fence. There was a hole about fifteen inches in diameter, which passed under the barrier.

"You see," the Gardener said, "how it burrowed deeply to avoid that part of the fence extending under the surface."

"What else could it do? You can't expect a grif to cut *concilium* wire. They have weak jaws and little strength generally. A grif competes against other animals with its cunning. It is not even good at running."

"Can they climb?"

"Fairly well. Not like a cat or squirrel. But not on these sharpened strands, in any case. They would cut its soft hide to bits. That's why it had to dig."

"Here are some footprints," said the Gardener.

"I saw them. This grif must be a male. The females have smaller feet. They are very scarce. That is why the race is doomed."

"Where will you put the trap?"

"I shall set one here at the end of the tunnel, where the grif must pass over it to get out. The other among the vegetables. Which kind did it like best?"

"There were many tomatoes missing, but they were most perfectly ripe. It also took lettuce and potatoes. Fruit, too."

"Then there isn't much choice. I'll set it here on the path. It's the one in the tunnel that I'm counting on, anyhow. Once you know which food a grif likes best, it is easy. We caught many in the old days who couldn't resist sweet things, like chocolate."

"Will the trap cause much pain?"

"That is hard to say. Grifs don't feel things the way our Master does. He is highly sensitive even to small variations of heat and pressure. A grif doesn't die very easily when badly injured, but may not feel a great deal of pain. Insects, they say, will keep on eating after their abdomens have been severed. But grifs were almost extinct when our Masters came to this world, so nobody really knows very much about them. As you see, the teeth of the trap are hollow needles which inject a powerful poison. On the whole, it is doubtful that this grif will suffer."

As the Gardener watched, the Custodian put the device in the mouth of the tunnel, and pressed a stud. With a faint whir the trap flattened itself against the soil, seeming to the casual gaze only an irregular greyish patch of earth.

"Won't the grif see it? The contrast is clear."

"To us, but not to them. They detect some colors well; others very poorly. I don't think it can see grey in the dark. At least, that's what the Chief Exterminator used to say years ago when I first came here."

"Well, we shall know tomorrow," the Gardener said thoughtfully.

But the next morning he made an indignant report.

"That grif," he complained to the Custodian. "It is not merely cunning, but malicious."

"What do you mean?"

"The trap is sprung, but caught nothing. The grif was evidently very angry, and deliberately ruined much more than it could carry off. I don't know how it got past the trap in the tunnel."

"Show me; I will understand."

The Gardener led the way. Outside the mouth of the passage they found the trap hunched in sprung position, bright needle teeth together, their tips dripping greenish venom. The Custodian studied the soft soil.

"I see," he said. "The grif must have used a stick. Obviously it sprung the trap that way, and then shoved it out of the opening. Only the most intelligent of the native fauna ever use even the simplest of tools."

"What about the other trap?"

"You see the footprints. The grif went slowly, prodding with the stick. Notice the little holes its tip made in the ground. If the grif had jabbed the trap, it would have seized the stick as before. Evidently it took a different path. After all, there are many ways to get at the vegetables. Since it doesn't care about trampling the crops, no path is necessary. As you said, though, much of this damage is obviously malicious destruction. That is the way of wild beasts. Some defile the traps or cover them with dirt; others slay livestock wantonly in anger. This one shows his hate of us and our defenses by uprooting plants. What was carried off this time?"

"Many different kinds. About twenty pounds altogether, perhaps. But he ruined fifty times as much."

"Look at this—a furrow on the earth. The grif filled a sack of some kind. A few of them can weave with vines like birds or spiders." He reflected a moment. "Perhaps we should fill the tunnel and then charge the fence."

"Electrify it?" the Gardener demanded.

"Why not? There is plenty of power. With the Master gone, many appliances are shut down. When the grif is dead, I can turn off the current again."

"It's your problem," said the Gardener. "I tend the soil. The Master does not expect me to catch grifs."

"I am aware of our respective responsibilities. Besides, it is obvious that your intelligence and training are inadequate for anything more than raising squash."

"That is true, provided you include fruits and grains. I am not a one-crop gardener, like some."

"I have decided," the Custodian said, ignoring the implied reproof. "The fence shall be charged by tonight. I should think that five thousand volts would be enough. All living cells are equally vulnerable to electrical coagulation or nervous fibrillation. Get back to your tomatoes, and leave this grif to me."

With the expert assistance of the maintenance staff, the Custodian led heavy silver wires from the nuclear generator to the wire fence. Permanent leads were available on each hundred-yard stretch, so that the job was quite easy. When the current was switched on, at dusk, the ten-foot barrier became lethal to any living thing that touched it. The Custodian displayed satisfaction. Undoubtedly a dead and well toasted grif would be found hanging there in the morning.

But at dawn the Gardener quickly disillusioned him.

"It got in again! More perfect crops ravaged! You must do something."

"How? It's not possible; the fence was charged."

"It made another tunnel. A deeper, longer one."

"But how could it do that without even touching the wires? The grif would search for the old passage first. Surely, the most natural thing in the world would be to touch, or accidentally brush, the fence."

"Well, it didn't. Come and see for yourself."

The Custodian examined the new shaft ruefully. It began some six feet beyond the wire, and went down at least four beneath the lowest of the buried strands. The job must have taken most of the night, even in soft loam.

"How did it know?" the Custodian wondered aloud.

"Listen," the Gardener admonished. "There are sound waves from the wires."

"That is true; we can detect them. But what does a brute know about electrical hum?"

"There is more. Test the soil."

"A small leakage of current; that is to be expected when so large a mass of metal is heavily charged."

"If we can detect it, why not the grif?"

The Custodian was momentarily at a loss.

"It is possible," was the reluctant admission. "There isn't much recorded on the grif's nervous system. You and I can easily detect a few millivolts. But I never suspected a grif might do it."

"It doesn't have to. The leakage near the fence amounts to almost thirty volts."

"Yes, that's true. I could reduce the loss, but that would take time. Besides, for all we know it is more sensitive to electricity than we are. Let's see what the prints outside the fence can tell us."

Beyond the enclosure they found further evidence that current leakage had alerted the grif. There were signs of a normal stride to within eight feet of the fence. Then the grif had stopped abruptly, retreated a few paces, and returned with great caution. Obviously its feet had tingled a warning.

"This grif is too wary for you," the Gardener complained. "There was much stolen and more destroyed last night. Many pounds of fine berries that were to be frozen today."

"No grif can escape for long," the Custodian reassured him. "I shall study the records and finish this matter soon. My mistake has been to draw on limited personal experience. Instead I must learn something in detail about the beast."

"Do it fast," the Gardener urged. "The Master might blame me if this damage is not stopped immediately. That is, if He ever returns," he added thoughtfully.

The next day, at morning report time, the Custodian gave the Gardener a brief, informal lecture on grifs.

"At one time they dominated this planet. Now there are only a few degenerate subspecies. The older types were very gregarious. Their main drives were for food and sex, although the early social forms also sought something called power. It meant giving orders, like our Master.

"Now I have an idea. We shall use one of the strongest of these urges to bait our trap. This male is almost certainly alone, since females are so scarce. It must want a mate desperately. Well, I shall offer it one."

"How can you do that?"

"With the aid of my technicians and what is known about the anatomy of the grif. Tomorrow morning, when you report, we shall be ready for the brute's evening raid."

"It's a fine job of design," said the Gardener admiringly. "But are you sure the grif cannot tell? What about odor? Or noise, like the hum of the wires."

"This is quite silent, since there is a minimum of movement required. Although the grif may have a better nose than we think, it is obvious that a wild beast picks up many smells on its person. It goes through fragrant herbs, gets covered with loamy soil, and even spills bits of food on its skin. But aside from that, I have anointed this trap with flower scents. They were once peculiar to the adult females, and among the social forms such odors drew the male to the other sex. Let us hope that this degenerate type will still respond. In any case, there are no suspicious odors involved."

Together they carried the trap out beyond the fence, and placed it upright in a natural pose, as if startled and tiptoe, ready to flee. Its pink, rounded contours gleamed in the sun; its breast rose and fell as if to breathing; it was soft and warm to the touch, and smelled of roses.

"It should be quite irresistible to a lonely, sex starved male," the Custodian said confidently.

"I could almost feel sorry for the grif," the Gardener replied.

"I don't know what you mean. Lately you make meaningless remarks. How does one feel sorry?"

"I can't explain it. It's just something I heard the Master say now and then. Like when his little child died. I don't know what it means, but it's supposed to apply to situations like this, when something dies that might have gone on living."

"Gone on crop stealing, you mean. Better stick to plants; as a philosopher you are not competent."

"At least, I am a good gardener. No tree of mine ever fails to produce the limit. Except," he added, "when insects or grifs interfere."

The night came, balmy and warm breathing. It was August, so the full moon hung low, burning in the clear sky. There were many scents in the breeze, woven through its texture like colored threads.

Then the grif appeared, walking pale and naked in the moonlight. It moved with great wariness, examining every inch of the ground ahead, stopping now and then to listen, and obviously ready to flee at any moment. It carried a crudely woven mesh sack over one shoulder.

When the grif was ten yards from the fence, it froze and tried to pierce the moon-shadows with its searching gaze. Something stood there, just a few feet away. It was slim and naked, a being strange, yet attractive. The heady scent of roses reached the grif's broad, flat nose, giving rise to new emotions that clawed him mercilessly. With caution he moved closer, and as he approached, the little head, with its streaming golden hair, turned towards him. The long eyelashes fluttered up to reveal large, brilliant eyes. She raised white arms yearningly, and he shrank back for a moment as though menaced. His feelings became unbearably poignant. Then he lost all restraint, all fear, all contact with the real world, and leaped forward to seize her …

They found him in the morning, dead in the arms of the decoy, his wiry, dirty body distorted from the lethal surge of current.

"You were right," the Gardener said. "The grif couldn't resist her. I don't know what drew it. I cannot understand. Why did he want to hold this thing in his arms so badly that he lost all caution?"

"That is something we will never really know. The Master understands; he had a mate. All living things feel it. We cannot expect to. Let us recover our trap. Who knows, some day another grif may come after your crops."

They pulled the dead man free, and the two robots, carrying the third, left.

Doomsday Incident

Inside information can be as trivial as a tip on a horse, or as important as survival itself. When Darryl Greenwood learned, well in advance of his community, that hydrogen bomb missiles would certainly be plunging down from the skies in less than two hours, his first thought was of the swimming pool; his second was a fervent feeling of gratitude for the tip, which came from a brother at the Pentagon.

There were good reasons for the irrational sequence: the money that might have made his shelter truly adequate had been diverted to the kidney-shaped depression of tepid water. He realized now, with dreadful clarity, that the pitiful beams and sandbags in his cellar would never do; that he and his were done for. Two hundred dollars for the shelter; six thousand for the pool—the ratio didn't seem so good at the moment.

Then the solution came. Nobody else knew about the missiles as yet. And just two houses down was the really splendid shelter of Les Pollock. Les, the cautious, cool one. No pool for him. "I'd rather be bone dry and breathing!" he'd told Greenwood. So he had a spot twenty feet down, in the center of a block of concrete and steel. It was carefully designed to provide for any emergency. Les had displayed its facilities with pride. If he was foolish to be so frank about its secrets, why, after all, he'd known Darryl for years. Besides, Greenwood had a shelter of his own, which might do very well for a fringe area like this one.

The line of action was quite obvious. Any minute now a public announcement might be made. After that, chaos, with Les dashing wildly from his store downtown to his home, there to lead his family into the shelter.

Greenwood's mind was racing like a well-oiled engine. Have Myra pick up the kids at school, while he went over to invade Pollock's shelter. Mrs. Pollock and the twins would almost certainly be out. That was good; he didn't fancy facing them, although if he had to, he could. Once in the shelter, the Pollocks could not possibly get them out in time. Les had explained the whole set-up. Only a wrecking crew with crowbars and explosives could crack the place in less than three or four hours—and by that time nobody outside would be able to try.

At zero minus eighty minutes, by Greenwood's estimate, he, Myra, and the kids swung the massive door shut. The Pollocks could barely have had the news by then; in any case, they were too late.

"They'll make us get out," Myra whimpered, her fatly pretty face full of distress. "I just know they will."

"They can't," Darryl said crisply. "There's no outside control; Les made that clear. He trusted his neighbors—maybe because we all had our own shelters," Greenwood added cynically.

Gordon, a thin, sullen boy, with hotly intolerant eyes, said: "He'll block the air pipes. At least, that's what I'd do."

"No, he won't," Darryl told his son. "Les was too careful. They're built in multiple, with the openings behind bends and things. Besides, there's a snake around here just for that. Where did he put it—ah—it's in that carton."

"I'm hungry," little Cathy whined. Her fat face, a miniature replica of Myra's, was grubby; a large drop hung from her flat nose. "Ma, I said I'm hungry."

Myra moved listlessly to the food cupboard, opened a large box, and fished out a thick cracker.

"That's the Swedish hardtack stuff Les told us about," Darryl said. "It keeps, and has a lot of food value."

Myra held it out to Cathy, who slapped it from her mother's hand.

"Do' wan' that. Gimme candy."

"There isn't any candy," Myra said, pawing the food stores in a halfhearted way. "Eat it, baby; it's good. See, watch Mama eat some."

"Do' wan' it! Wan' candy." The child was wailing now.

"For God's sake," Darryl said, reaching into his pocket. He pulled out a half melted chocolate bar, and tossed it to Cathy.

Gordon gave an audible sniff, his pale eyes full of contempt.

"How long must we stay here?" Myra asked, addressing the question to nobody in particular.

"Depends," Darryl said. "If it's a bad attack, we may have to stay down here for six weeks. Even with a light one, at least two weeks."

"What will happen to Les and Shirley?" Myra demanded.

"How the hell do I know?" He glared at her. "Do you think I like doing this to them? I'm doing it for you; me, I'd take my chances at home."

"Sure," Gordon said in his sharply nasal voice. "It's for us, Ma. When he got old Professor Kogan fired by those anonymous letters, that was for us, too. He didn't want Kogan's job—not at all. He needed it for us."

"You shut up," Darryl snapped. "Pity you can't use some of that sarcasm in your themes and get a passing grade now and then. The English teacher says you write like a third grader instead of a high school freshman."

At that moment they became aware of a faint rapping on the thick door, and the murmur of a voice.

"That's Les and Shirley," Myra said, licking her lips.

"Can hardly hear 'em," Darryl said. "That's really a door. No wonder this place cost all that money."

"He said not to get that pool," Myra said. "We should have listened."

"Don't try to blame me," Darryl cried. "Who the hell pestered me for weeks? All of you wanted it. I hardly got to use it, what with the kids' pals in it night and day."

The pounding on the door was louder now, with a kind of desperate urgency that could be sensed rather than heard.

"Must be using a club of some kind," Greenwood muttered. "Much good that'll do him."

"What if he gets a couple of big insecticide bombs and sprays the hell out of us through the air openings?" Gordon asked. "Ever think of that?"

For a moment Darryl seemed to shrink; then his face brightened.

"I remember now. There's pressure in here from the minute I started the conditioner. Nothing can blow in for long; all the air that comes in is filtered, and the used part pumped out. That's to keep out the poison from the bomb."

"So the poor boob's really had it," Gordon said. "Well played, Dad!"

Darryl looked at him suspiciously, but the thin face was wooden. Only the light, grey eyes were smoldering. Kids, Greenwood thought angrily. He'd given the boy everything: his own car; pocket money; the pool. But he was worthless at school; never had a job—hell with him. The boy seemed to hate him at times. What father tried harder?

The pounding stopped. There was silence outside.

"Guess he knows that can't help," Darryl said. He looked at his watch. "Any minute now. I hope to God they don't miss L.A. and hit near here. Nothing could take that, they say."

Myra was chalk white, and sat down as if her joints were water. Gordon was fiddling with the transistor radio.

Suddenly they heard a strange pattering sound. From several of the air vents shining globules rained to the concrete floor, where they rolled, scattering into tiny spheres that raced about as if alive.

"What the devil—!" Darryl said.

Another silver shower followed; every part of the floor, every corner, every crack or crevice, had its pin points of gleaming metal.

Cathy pursued one large drop with shrieking glee, trying to seize it. But it easily eluded her grasp; the stuff could not be held at all.

Darryl was staring at the floor in wonder.

"It came through the air pipes," he muttered. "It must be Les—but why? What good will that do him?"

Gordon stooped to study the stuff; a muscle in his cheek was twitching. He began to laugh: a hoarse, humorless croak. He looked squarely at his father.

"We've really had it," he said. "That's mercury."

"Mercury?" Darryl's expression was one of blank bewilderment.

"That's right, mercury—quicksilver. He must have broken that big barometer he was so nuts about."

"But why—what good—?"

"What good? He's finished us, that's all. This stuff is deadly poison; our science teacher told us about it. Only time old Creepy had anything interesting to say."

"What do you mean, poison?" Darryl asked. "We can clean it up; get it out through the disposal."

"That's what you think. You couldn't gather it up in weeks; and in a closed place like this, there'll be enough evaporating in the air to kill us all long before we can get out."

"The filters—"

"They can't get all that mercury out of here," Gordon insisted. "He must've poured down a pound of the stuff."

It was then that they felt the earth shake; and even in their concrete block they seemed to feel a transient flash of enormous radiant energy. Almost immediately there were other shocks. Some cartons fell with a crash. Cathy was wailing with a shrillness unusual even for her. The last tremor died away.

"Not too close," Darryl said. "Thank God."

Gordon walked slowly to the door; he put one hand on the heavy steel bar.

"Like I said," he told them, almost absently. "No use staying here. There won't be any doctors to spare, and anyhow they can't help with mercury."

"Get away from that door!" Darryl cried. "You damn fool kid; what d'you know? D'you think I'd open up just because of some silly ideas you have about this stuff?" He scuffed his feet among the silver globules; they rolled in all directions like terrified animalculae.

Gordon wrenched at the bar, but before he could budge it, his father leaped at him. There was a brief struggle, and the boy was flung back. Greenwood stood in front of the door, panting.

"I can still handle a punk like you," he said thickly. "We're staying here at least two weeks—if no more bombs fall."

"By then we'll have enough mercury in us so it won't matter," Gordon said, his pale eyes hot with anger and contempt. "God, I wish Les Pollock was my father."

After staying silent for some time, his mother spoke.

144

"That's a terrible thing to say," she told him heavily. "Maybe you'd like Shirley for a mother, too."

"Stop that, both of you," Darryl ordered. "By God, we're a family, and let's stay that way. If a few decent people survive, there's always hope for the world. Some of our kind will be left when it's all over."

Gordon was staring at the shiny globes of mercury. "That's right," he said, half to himself. "Not us—not now—but plenty of our kind."

The shelter was quivering again; the earth shuddered like some great beast in agony. Cathy screamed and screamed.

Priceless Possession

When Lieutenant Garret got the summons from the Control Room, his first thought was that the captain had died. What else could account for the excited note in the ensign's voice? He swung himself out of his berth, zipped through the passage and snapped: "What is it, Luis? Drug no good? Is the Captain—"

Alvarez looked at him so blankly that Garret bit off the end of his question.

"Drug?" the boy repeated. He seemed almost dazed. "No, it's not the Skipper. I wanted permission to change course. You'll think I'm crazy, Lieutenant, but so help me, we're almost ramming an S-2. It's hardly four degrees off our course-vector."

"An S-2! We should be that lucky! The last was taken eleven—no, fourteen years ago. You must be hallucinating, boy."

"That's what I figured at first. But the sail began to show up on the micro-screen. A big one, if I'm not seeing things. Damned big."

He heard the lieutenant whistle softly, and knew why.

In 1870, a whaler—or beachcomber—who found a large chunk of that mysterious substance, ambergris, was a fortunate fellow, sure to make a lot of money from his discovery. In 2270, a comparable but even rarer and more valuable windfall was the taking of an S-2, or Solar Sailor.

The first had been spotted in 2164. It knocked the world of science off balance for years to follow. The notion that any organism could live and grow in airless, irradiated, non-temperatured space was so novel and hard to accept that the crew of the *Hakluyt* were long called hoaxers, who with fake photos were amusing themselves at the public's expense.

However, after several more of the weird creatures had been seen, the evidence built up beyond doubting. It was no longer possible to deny the truth.

The S-2, like the Portuguese Man of War of Earth's seas, consists of a jellylike body from which sprouts a sail that reacts to the pressure of light. The organism apparently lives by ingesting cosmic dust much as whales utilize plankton. It can furl or twist its sail—something never observed, but inferred—but quite slowly, having no muscles as such, and so guides its movement in space. Obviously, it must avoid getting trapped in a strong gravitational field, since it could never escape, and would either crash on a planet or be immolated in a sun. Of necessity, it cruises only where the impact of photons against the sail dominates the pull of matter.

Since all attempts to communicate with the organism were failures, the Galactic Council reluctantly classified it as a lower animal of inconsiderable consciousness, and lawful game.

As for the sail, the source of the creature's commercial value, it is the most remarkable fabric to be found in the whole galaxy, and almost beyond price. Thin and light as the finest spider-silk, it is stronger than the toughest synthetics, from nylon-gamma to durette; and can be cut only with power shears of *concilium* alloy. It is fireproof, waterproof and unaffected by any chemical reagent, however concentrated. It is also a near-perfect conductor of electricity, having a resistance close to zero at all temperatures. Finally, the material shimmers rainbowlike under radiation of every wavelength, from cosmic rays to the longest members of the AM band. Whether for the most precise instruments or the gowns of multimillionaire women, the fabric is so much in demand, and so scarce, that the price must be set by public auction.

Every attempt at duplication in the laboratory failed; and it is thought that the missing factor may be time. It might take an S-2 a thousand years to grow its sail, one molecule at a time, under the rays of many classes of stars, in the hard vacuum of space—and such conditions aren't to be simulated in any laboratory.

The note of excitement in Alvarez's voice was now accounted for. Aside from the basic drama of the find, the boy saw barriers dropping in all directions. He saw, too, in his mind's eye, the lovely face of Julia Marlowe, whose father was a senior member of the Galactic Council, and not likely to let his daughter marry a penniless ensign. She was fond enough of the boy, approving his darkly handsome face and muscular body; but she spent more on cosmetics and perfume than he earned. She was beautiful, gay, generous and sweet, but there was plenty of her father's iron in the girl, and she would never settle down to live on love alone.

But now that he was about to be one-third owner of a huge S-2 sail ...

Garret had been studying the image on the screen, his pale, glittering eyes a glacial blue.

"You're right, by God—I didn't believe it until this minute! Luis, do you know what that lovely beastie out there means to us?"

The lieutenant knew what it meant to *him*, all right. He was over age in grade, and soon to be retired on the usual pittance. A first rate fighting man, brave, quick witted and up to every dirty dodge of battle, it was only his lack of self-control that kept him from climbing. Thickset, blocky, with hot, intolerant eyes, he always preferred a blow to a word: tops in a messy brawl, but never seeing more than ten minutes ahead.

"Do I?" the ensign replied to Garret's question. "It means about a million credits, at least—a three-way split. If the Captain lives," he added quickly. "And then I can ask Julia to marry me."

"Good for you," the lieutenant said, only half hearing. He was thinking what his own share would do. No more worry about living on his retirement pay, or taking some job that exploited his former rank and cluster of decorations. A life of luxury was now the prognosis: wine, women—he could do without song; the rustle of large denomination bills was the most musical sound of all.

"Well," Alvarez said, grinning hugely. "What are we waiting for? They say a laser beam in that big bluish spot just off center kills the thing dead. And no risk of hurting the sail—as if anything could."

"Right. Move in now. We should be within range in an hour. The first in fourteen years," he murmured gloatingly. "They may be practically extinct, even with the few taken. Or bunched up in some other galaxy; the ones captured here might be real wanderers." He made some careful measurements with the micrometers, and said in an exultant voice: "I make the dimensions of this sail as giving five hundred square feet. And it should bring in a lot more than the last, because they've gone without so long. Million credits, hell—if this doesn't net us twice that at the auction, I'll eat the jelly part—no bread!"

The ensign manipulated the controls, and the ship began to converge on the S-2. Then the captain's voice, weak but lucid, came over the intercom.

"Lieutenant Garret," it said. "Please come to my quarters at once. Alvarez, too."

"Say," the boy said. "The new drug's working. He sounds fine. Kill or cure, the medicos said, and they were right. He'd be dead without it—you saw how bad he was."

"This is a lucky day all around," the lieutenant said. "One quickie course in Medical Techniques, and you save the Skipper's life; not bad. Well, put the ship on auto again, and let's go. This news ought to complete the cure."

When they came in, Captain Ling was struggling to a sitting position; his eyes were feverishly bright, and he panted.

"There's Something outside," he gasped. "It's been communicating with me—mentally."

They gaped at him.

"What is?" the boy demanded.

"An S-2," the captain said. "Didn't you spot it? What kind of a watch you two keeping while I—never mind. Maybe it's still too far off. Anyhow, it was telling a friend: 'I'm going to die soon; the Killers are near, and must have detected me. We can't communicate with them, and they always destroy us; I don't know why. Goodbye—' I didn't get the other's name, if it has one. It was so far away … another galaxy, I think. Yet they were in touch instantly."

"You're hallucinating, Captain," Garrett said. "You know very well that nobody's ever talked to an S-2. They're just space jellyfish—lower animals. Weird and wonderful, but no more intelligent than a worm."

149

Ling propped himself up, lips narrowing.

"Is there an S-2 out there or not?"

"Yes, sir," the lieutenant admitted reluctantly. He gave the captain a lowering stare. "Telepathy is known to occur among humans. It's not subject to control, but does exist. You must have caught some of my thoughts—or Luis'. That has to be it."

Ling looked bewildered; he was still very ill, and not thinking clearly. He sank back in his bunk, breathing heavily.

"Maybe you're right, but we must be sure. Don't kill it; you mustn't. That's an order," he said, his voice hardening.

"But, Captain," his exec protested. "The S-2 is officially classified as a lower animal, subject to capture—legitimate game. Your order is actually illegal. I don't have to remind you, sir, what such a find is worth. Your share would be at least—"

"Never mind that," Ling snapped. "I'm in command, Lieutenant. If an order's illegal, you know the regulations: obey it, and complain later. I shouldn't have to point that out to an officer of your experience."

"But we'll lose the thing!" Garret said angrily. "Maybe you don't care, but I'm not passing up a fortune—one of the few a serviceman can get. Everything else the civvies latch on to, while we must settle for wages!"

Ling's eyes widened at Garret's tone, but he merely said quietly: "You can follow it for a while. Maybe I can make contact again."

"I'm sure it was the new drug, Captain," Alvarez suggested. "You were so far gone we took a chance on that new stuff—the psychic energizer. It gave you hallucinations."

"But it was all so clear—and logical," Ling said, almost to himself. "They live very slowly compared to us, sailing from one universe to another—across those incredible gaps we haven't dared to tackle yet. They avoid matter; maybe that's why we've found so few. They daren't get trapped by a gravity field. That small mass of theirs—it takes millennia to build up from cosmic dust down into usable food. Their thoughts are too sluggish for us, and their motions, too. They just can't signal in time to ask our mercy. Helpless—it's a terrible thing. If only I could slow my thinking down to match ... we

150

can record speech, and run that at any speed, but thought ..." He closed his eyes.

"Just how will you make contact, then?" Garret demanded sullenly. "We can't follow it forever; we have a deadline of our own. Rigel III by next month, remember?"

"I don't know," the captain admitted, without opening his eyes. "I'm all muddled up right now. Nothing's coming through at the moment." Then his lids snapped up. "There's only one way, but it's obvious enough. You'll have to give me more of the new drug."

"But, Captain," Alvarez objected. "That's risky. You were lucky once. Why push it?"

"I have to. If that's the stuff to stir up nerve endings or get them synchronized somehow with an S-2's thoughts, I have to try it. I won't have it on my conscience that I let a highly intelligent being get killed by my crew. And a noble being, too. If you could have felt its personality! No hatred of us; a pure spirit ..."

"I'd be pure, too, just floating alone in space," Garret said sourly. "But I have to live on Earth, and that costs money."

"You don't know what you're saying," Ling said. "You're not that callous. And there's more. They can't *do* anything; no organs for manipulation, but what minds! I could hear this one; he was building up a mathematical system. My specialty—and he lost me after the first five postulates! Think what we could learn! The theorem he was working towards would have unified electricity, gravitation, magnetism, elasticity, the nucleus—sounds wild, but I believe. I really do believe!"

"Not all math has practical significance," Garret said.

"Granted. But consider this one point. They've licked the communications problem. By some kind of thought exchange they converse over distances we can hardly conceive. When one buds— that's how they reproduce—the two drift apart for maybe fifty thousand years. The acceleration may be only .000001 meters per second squared, but you know how that builds up the velocity in time—simple integration. Yet father—and—call it 'son'—have no trouble talking across the void. Think how we need such a technique. Light's too slow for anything out of the piddling solar system itself.

And we're stymied with it." He sat up again, jaw out. "I don't have to convince you, damn it. Ensign—give me the drug again: that's an order!"

There was no resisting the command, not in this navy. The boy looked at Garret, who scowled, then shrugged.

When the second dose had been injected, the two men waited impatiently for a reaction. It came more quickly this time.

As soon as the captain began to recover, he said: "I'll prove it to you. If I can receive from the S-2, it can receive from me. I'll—I'll ask it to signal."

"Captain, that's crazy," said Garret. "What kind of signal could it give? It can't talk. It can't shoot off flares …"

"I'll ask it to furl its sail."

Garret hesitated. "We'll watch," he promised.

And watch they did, for hours, while the prospect of the money began to grow larger in both their minds.

"A million credits," said Alvarez.

"More than that. Twice that much."

"And it's all out there waiting for us. Can't get away. Wonder if it's smart enough to run anyway? Not that it could; you move pretty slow, sailing that way, with just a push from light-beams. It's as good as ours, no matter what. Two million credits—ooh!"

Then he gulped, staring at the micrometer dial, which was zeroed in on the sail's upper right hand corner. "Oh, no!"

"What?" the lieutenant barked, bringing his thoughts back from a pleasure palace on Rigel II, where a little money bought delights unknown on Earth.

"It's furling! So help me God, it is—look! We'd better tell the Captain right away."

He reached for the intercom, but Garret put a thick hand on his wrist.

"Hold it a minute. We need to make sure. Give it more time—while we talk."

But for many minutes they said nothing; just stared as the sail, curling very slowly, as a flower might, began to bring one corner down. After the motion left no doubt, Alvarez stirred restlessly; again the lieutenant restrained him.

"Listen," he said. "I'll make this linear—not a curve. And strictly negative on the memory cube. I'll deny saying it, officially." His dark face was grim. "All right; the thing's signaling; it has some sense. But it's not human—not like us; just a damned jellyfish. No matter what the Single Universe cloudheads say, I don't call every weird blob my brother just because it knows the multiplication table! There's a fortune out there, a real life for us. Gonna let it get away?"

"B—but," the boy stammered. "What about communication? That's just as valuable. We could make a pile."

"We? Don't be stupid! The lab boys would have to work tirelessly on the S-2 for years, maybe. And after they get the idea, how long to duplicate it? And who knows even if the drug would act the same on another guy? We could have long, grey beards before it's all worked out—and still have no claim, either." He gave the ensign a steady, cold stare. "I'll talk to the Captain; you back me—okay?"

Alvarez hesitated briefly, then said: "Okay."

"Let's go down; we can talk some more on the way."

They entered the cabin, and Ling peered at them.

"Sick," he mumbled. "Damned stuff hits my guts now." He managed to sit up. "Well? What happened? You must have seen it. The S-2 told me it had furled."

"I'm sorry, Captain," Garret said, his face open and honest, gaze steady. "Nothing happened. We watched very closely. Not the slightest sign of a signal. In fact, the thing opened its sail further and was moving off our course—running away, obviously. Or trying to; but it's just too slow. An animal reaction, I'd say. Lower animal escaping instinctively. You had hallucinations from that drug. Right, Alvarez?"

His face pale, the boy said: "That's right, Captain. No sign of any intelligent response. You must have dreamed up the whole exchange. It's a pity," he sighed.

"I should have known," Ling said bitterly, settling back in his bunk. "Some mighty good men tried to communicate—like Duclaux of the old *Josiah Willard Gibbs*—and couldn't get through. Just a drug, after all. Well," he said, looking at them owlishly, "I've held up your jackpot long enough. Go get your millions!"

"*Our* jackpot," Garret said. "And it's a big one, Captain. Your share will buy you that estate you've mentioned so often—that, and a whole lot more."

"I'd sooner have found what I thought was out there. But at least my conscience is clear."

Outside the cabin, the two officers exchanged glances.

"*His* conscience is clear," the lieutenant said. "And mine isn't worth two-thirds of a million credits." He put his hand on the boy's shoulder. "Your people have a saying I like: 'Take what you want—and pay for it.' "

"I know that one," Alvarez said wryly. "My father uses it quite a bit. And then Mother tells him: 'Ah, but when the bill finally comes, it may be too high.' " For a moment, as he spoke, his face, normally round and boyish, seemed old.

"On the other hand, sometimes the bill never comes," Garret said.

Checklist of Sources

Note: The checklist below gives the original publication source for each of the stories included in this collection, with the exception of "Doomsday Incident" which is published here for the first time.

"A Specimen for the Queen"
The Magazine of Fantasy and Science Fiction, May 1960

"Turning Point"
The Magazine of Fantasy and Science Fiction, September 1965

"The Rescuer"
Analog, July 1962

"Problem Child"
Analog, April 1964

"The Topper"
Analog, February 1963

"Controlled Experiment"
Analog, August 1963

"The Formula"
Amazing Stories, July 1963

"Degree Candidate"
Fantastic, January 1961

"The Auto Hawks"
Amazing Stories, September 1960

"Revenge"
Amazing Stories, February 1961

"Off His Rocker"
Fantastic, February 1960

"Mulberry Moon"
Fantastic, April 1961

"The Melanas"
Fantastic, December 1960

"A Civilized Community"
Bizarre! Mystery Magazine, October 1965

"Alien"
Rascal, September 1964

"Irresistible Attraction"
Rascal, November 1964

"Priceless Possession"
Galaxy, June 1966

About the Author

Arthur Porges was born in Chicago, Illinois on August 20, 1915. One of four brothers, he was educated at Roosevelt High School and Senn High School before enrolling at The Lewis Institute where he achieved a Bachelor of Science Degree in Mathematics. After the successful completion of his postgraduate studies, through which he attained Masters Degrees in Mathematics and Engineering from the Illinois Institute of Technology, Porges enlisted in the U.S. Army in 1942. During the Second World War he served as an artillery instructor, teaching algebra and trigonometry to field personnel. He was stationed at various military installations including Camp White in Oregon, Fort Sill, Oklahoma, Camp Roberts, California and at Barnes Hospital in Vancouver, Washington. After the war Porges returned to Illinois and taught mathematics at the Western Military Academy, going on to serve as an assistant professor at De Paul University. Having taught at Occidental College in Los Angeles for a brief stint in the late forties, Porges made a permanent move to California in 1951 and spent several years as a mathematics teacher at Los Angeles City College. During this period he wrote and sold short stories as a sideline. In 1957, Porges retired from teaching to write full-time. He went on to publish hundreds of short stories in numerous magazines and newspapers. Many of his stories appeared in *Alfred Hitchcock's Mystery Magazine*, *Ellery Queen's Mystery Magazine*, *Amazing Stories* and *The Magazine of Fantasy and Science Fiction*. His fiction spanned several genres, with tales ranging from science fiction and fantasy to horror, mysteries, and so on. At his most prolific his work was appearing in three or four periodicals in one month alone. Among his best-known stories are "The Ruum," "The Rats," "No Killer Has Wings," "The Mirror" and "The Rescuer." Nine previous book collections of his short stories have been published: *Three Porges Parodies and a Pastiche* (1988), *The Mirror and Other Strange*

Reflections (2002), *Eight Problems in Space: The Ensign De Ruyter Stories* (2008), *The Adventures of Stately Homes and Sherman Horn* (2008), *The Calabash of Coral Island and Other Early Stories* (2008), *The Miracle of the Bread and Other Stories* (2008), *The Devil and Simon Flagg and Other Fantastic Tales* (2009), *The Curious Cases of Cyriack Skinner Grey* (2009) and *The Ruum and Other Science Fiction Stories* (2010). A keen birdwatcher and an avid reader, in later years Porges wrote many articles, essays and poems, most of which were published in the *Monterey Herald*. Several of his poems were collected in the book *Spring, 1836: Selected Poems* (2008). After spells in Laguna Beach and San Clemente, Porges moved north, eventually settling in Pacific Grove. He passed away, at the age of 90, in May 2006.

www.ingramcontent.com/pod-product-compliance
Lightning Source LLC
Chambersburg PA
CBHW020134180626
46810CB00004B/1559